Beth Montgomery grew up in Melbourne.
She worked as a teacher in the
Pacific Islands and is married with
two children. *The Birthmark*
is her first novel.

the birthmark
beth montgomery

text publishing melbourne australia

The Text Publishing Company
Swann House
22 William Street
Melbourne Victoria 3000
Australia
www.textpublishing.com.au

First published in 2006

Design by Chong
Map by Bill Wood
Typeset in 10.5/14.7 Minister by J&M Typesetting
Printed and bound by Griffin Press

National Library of Australia
Cataloguing-in-Publication data:

Montgomery, Beth, 1965– .
The birthmark.

ISBN: 1 921145 33 1.

ISBN 13: 978 1 921145 33 9

I. Title.

A823.4

This project was assisted by the Commonwealth Government through
the Australian Council, its art funding and advisory body.

Australia **Council**
for the Arts

To Jezeloni, in memory of Yesterday

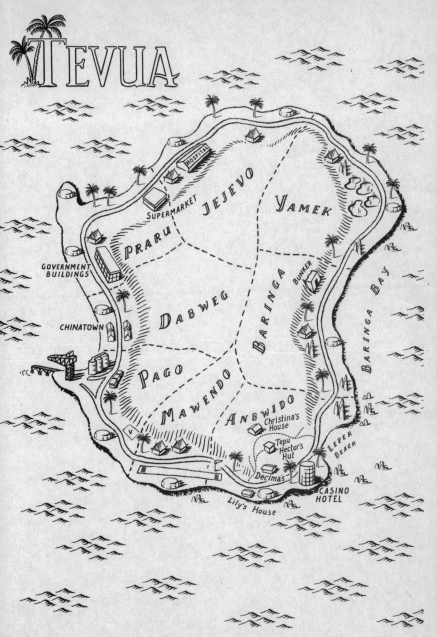

THE ISLAND OF TEVUA, PACIFIC OCEAN

one

Tepu disliked them from the moment he saw them. They had pale faces and thin bones. Their uniforms were light brown and contrasted with their black boots which had separate big toes. It made them look cloven-hoofed, like devils. They shouted at him, rushed at him, told him to get off his bicycle, at least that's what Tepu thought they were saying.

He jumped from the frame and let the bike weave and wobble towards them. The first soldier caught it just as it was about to fall. He righted it, then mounted the bike himself and rode off in jerky movements in the direction Tepu had just come from.

Tepu picked himself up from the road and shouted out after him, 'My bicycle! It's my bicycle!'

His insolence was met with a sharp blow to the face. The other two soldiers shouted at him and forced his head down.

That's how Tepu learnt to bow.

Rumours spread all over the island. Some said the soldiers were marines who had come for the phosphate. Others said it was to do with the war and that Tevua was to be a strategic Japanese outpost in the middle of the Pacific. Tepu doubted that story. They were too far away from other islands for a start, and it was unsafe for ships; the reef was broad and treacherous, without easy access to the shore. Lacking a natural harbour, Tevua was worthless as a military centre.

It was true that their island was full of phosphate, so Tepu thought this rumour was more likely. He hoped they would just take what they needed, then go. After all, what would the Japanese want with the people here?

Tepu knew they were dangerous. He decided to visit the leper colony to warn Edouwe and her family about the evil invaders and to tell her to be vigilant.

The colony was only ten minutes walk from his village, Anbwido. Set above the sloping beaches of the southeast of Tevua, at the edge of Baringa Bay, it consisted of twelve small bush huts and a clinic. Coconut palms and beach almonds fringed the camp and large coral pinnacles stood at the tide line like ancient stone statues.

He'd first met Edouwe on the beach there last year. Her shy smile had captivated him. Like most Tevuans, she was short and thickset with soft, rounded features. Her thick wavy hair fell to her waist, but was always held back from her face with a shell comb.

Tepu wondered if she would ever take any notice of him, a foreigner. Tepu's family were from the Gilbert

Islands, a thousand miles east, and the physical differences were obvious. The Gilbertese were taller and leaner than the Tevuans, their noses more prominent, and their hair was straight. There had been marriages between the two groups before, so Tepu thought he might have a chance.

Over the months, he'd made a point of fishing near the leper camp regularly, and they'd begun to talk. She was only fifteen, and even though she was not a leper herself, she was staying at the camp to look after her grandparents who had been sick with leprosy for many years.

Tepu had few relatives left alive on Tevua since the drought in the mid-1930s. Most had returned to the Gilbert Islands during those long years of hardship. Now his mother and younger brother were all that remained after his father had been lost at sea in a storm two years ago. Neither his body nor the canoe had ever been found.

In recent months Edouwe's grandparents had become like a second family to Tepu, sharing their stories, food and tobacco. He brought them fresh fish whenever he was successful with his net.

As he neared the leper colony, Tepu could see smoke from the kitchens rising against the background shimmer of the sea.

'Tepuariki, come and eat!' Edouwe's grandmother called out from the shade of one of the huts. He waved and hurried towards her. The old woman greeted him and offered him some dried fish. Even in the shadows he could see the gnarled pink knobs that were once her fingers, clasping the bowl awkwardly.

Tepu knew leprosy was the natural consequence of offending the island spirits. It was known on Tevua as the sickness of rotting flesh and it was a sad fate for those who had been cursed with it, but it was nothing to fear.

He smiled at her and ate some of the fish. He couldn't imagine what she had done to earn the island spirits' wrath.

'What news, Tepu?' she asked.

He told her about the Japanese, how they had stolen his bike and shouted at him. 'Many more have now come to Tevua. They have guns and swords and some of them have beaten people, rounded them up and forced them to move to the other side of the island,' he said. 'It's not safe, Mele,' he warned, looking around as if the enemy were nearby. 'Where is Edouwe? She must stay with you all the time and not walk to town alone.'

'She's gathering coconuts on the far side of Anbwido. She'll return soon.' The old woman nodded to reassure him.

Tepu hoped she was right. He didn't want anything to happen to Edouwe, not just because he admired her, but especially since he had begun to think that she was also fond of him. He had seen the shine in her eyes, caught the gentle smile she sent his way and his heart swelled.

Hector hunched over his plate of meat and rice, shovelling it into his mouth in neat handfuls. The Chinese couple who ran the tin shed restaurant watched him from behind the counter. Oblivious to their attention, he wiped the sweat from his face with the bottom of his T-shirt.

He wanted to hunt for chickens in the forest between the restaurant and Government Settlement. He knew the area well: all the bush tracks, who lived in which house, all the rocks, trees and coral pinnacles that formed natural hiding spots. Some would say he knew the area too well. It was a great place to catch chickens because the 'expats' were hardly ever home, and if they were, they didn't lay claim to any of the chickens wandering around. It was unlike other parts of the island where an angry householder would catch you by the neck if you poached one of their fowls.

Footsteps at the restaurant entrance made Hector look up. It was Lily Fasiti, the girl he'd thought about too much lately. She strode in and made her way to the counter, her thongs slapping loudly on the worn lino.

'One fish rice!' she called to the cooks, then turned and surveyed the room, stark with its pale blue walls and scrubbed laminated tables. Her eyes narrowed as she saw Hector in the corner.

'Looking for flies in your black bean meat?' she asked.

Hector chuckled and felt his face blush. Why was she

talking to him? He hardly knew her, except as an easy target to throw things at on the school bus. He was even more surprised when she slumped into the bench opposite him and sighed. Too afraid to look directly at her for long, he glanced up and noticed her eyes. They were heavy and bloodshot.

'What's happening?' he asked, unsure of what else to say.

'Same as always.'

Hector nodded, even though he had no idea what she meant. He was aware of her watching his thin fingers picking at the rice. He wondered what to say next. He'd never really had a conversation with a teenage girl before. They all thought he was hideous. The scar on his face made sure of that; everyone winced the first time they saw him. His grandfather always said it was because people imagined the pain he must have endured having his face savaged by a dog. Hector knew it was because he looked revolting.

More and more self-conscious, he stared at his food in an effort to hide his scar from Lily. But she didn't seem to care. Perhaps because in her own way she was just as disfigured as he was. Her left hand was stained purple, all the way to the elbow. Hector used to think it looked weird, but after seeing it so often he'd almost forgotten about it. No one, however, got used to his face.

Lily shifted uneasily on the bench, looked around and drummed her fingers against the tabletop.

'What's wrong, you hiding from someone?' he asked.

She took a long time to answer. 'Yeah, maybe,' she said

finally in an amused tone. 'Maybe you can help me escape.'

'Huh?'

'Are you going looking for things today?' she asked him quietly.

Hector was startled by her question. What did she mean, looking for things, thieving maybe? 'I'm looking for chickens,' he said defensively.

'Who with?' she asked. It was a dumb question. Everyone knew Hector was usually alone.

'Just me—want to come?'

'What would I do with a chicken?' she laughed. 'Yeah, why not? Let's go.' She slid out from the bench and walked to the entrance.

'Don't you want your food?' Hector said.

'Forget it.'

Hector pushed his plate aside and ran after her.

The cook scurried out from behind the counter waving a wooden spoon. 'Pay! Pay! You no pay!' she howled as she charged to the door. But the two of them had vanished into the protection of the forest.

'Hurry, she'll catch you!' Hector shouted. He'd overtaken Lily in just a few strides, his skinny legs used to fleeing. 'She's right behind you,' he teased, knowing full well that the Chinese woman had given up pursuing them. Lily crashed through the undergrowth behind him, a look of terror on her face.

Hector stopped running and doubled up with laughter.

'What's so funny?' she screeched, almost bowling him over in her effort to escape.

'She won't follow—they never do.'

She pushed Hector so hard that he toppled sideways. '*Ngaitirre!* Don't trick me—ever,' she swore.

He was still laughing when he hit the ground and Lily laughed too then.

'Where are we going, chicken boy?' she asked, breathless.

'Along the Witch Track. If you cut through the bush you come out near Government Settlement.'

'Why go there? White people don't have any chickens.'

'No, but that's where all the best Tevua chickens go.'

'Why?'

'Because they like the white people, they like vanilla better than chocolate.'

She laughed at his little joke as they walked along the track. Hector listened to her throaty chuckle. It made him feel good to think that she accepted him. *She* didn't treat him like dog shit. *She* could look him in the eye and not turn away.

After a few minutes he led her off the trail onto a thickly forested rise. Bean trees heavy with drops of moisture hung over the main canopy of tree hibiscus and the occasional coconut. Inside, the light was dim, and Hector could only see specks of blue through the forest above. He stopped at the base of a bean tree. The spreading buttress of the tree was like the back of an armchair; he sat and leant against it.

'Sit first,' he said.

'Why?'

'To listen. You have to listen and be still. Then you know where they are.'

He looked up at her legs, marked with scars. He'd often admired their strength and tone. He liked the chains of colourful beads and the black rubber rings from oilcans that covered her ankles. He liked her honey-brown skin; it was a shade lighter than most Tevuans. He liked her round unblemished face and he liked her fearlessness. He liked a lot about this girl. If only she knew. He turned his head before she could see his face darken.

Lily moved away from him, crouched to pick up a small stick and started to scratch in the black soil.

'Sssss,' he hissed at her, 'can't hear them scratch when you're scratching, too.'

Lily spat in the dirt, then curled her top lip at him. Just like her mum, Hector thought, that mean woman from the Works Department.

'Bastard!' she said laughing, and she threw the stick at him.

'*Suh!* Sit down and shut up.'

She sat and pulled her skirt tightly over her knees. Knees for me, Hector smiled, then turned away. He had to switch from looking at her to hunting.

He stared into the scrub behind the buttress. Black and copper shadows and outlines of tangled forms whispered to him. He watched for falling leaves above and the movement of small black crabs in the dappled undergrowth below. Silence grew easily between them.

'Listen to the forest,' he murmured.

Soon, into the silence came the gentle rhythmic

flicking of black soil onto dry leaves. Hector rummaged in his pockets and pulled out a coil of string and a pocket-knife. Lily frowned at him. He tilted his head towards the scrub, indicating the approaching quarry.

'They're here. Go get a young coconut,' he whispered, pointing to a nearby clump of shoots. 'But quiet, and hurry.'

She uprooted the nearest seedling and shook the soil away from the husk.

Hector set to work unravelling the string to make a snare. He crept into the clearing and placed the trap on the ground, covering it with dead leaves and loose soil.

As Lily brought the coconut over, the scratching noises stopped. The hens were suspicious. Hector took the coconut from Lily and prised open the brown husk with his knife. He stuck his blade in the pale yellow spongy kernel and discarded the rest of the seedling. He snapped off a chunk of kernel then held the rest out for Lily to take some.

'Spit it out, don't eat it all,' he whispered.

'It smells like soap, but it tastes so sweet,' she said as she chewed. Then she copied Hector and spat the tiny shards onto a large curled leaf he'd found at the base of their hiding tree.

Once they'd produced enough bait, he spread most of it in the snare and sprinkled a trail near the bush where the chicken noises had come from.

They hid again and waited for what seemed like hours. Hector's knees burned with pain as he squatted behind the bean tree.

Soon he was rewarded. Three chickens emerged into the clearing, following the baited trail. They moved steadily along, peck, peck, pecking. Closer and closer they came until the red one in front reached the hidden snare. She scratched at the soil, unearthing the end of a stick and a section of the twine. She paused, turned, then rushed at the main heap of coconut in the centre of the snare.

Hector held his breath. He could feel a surge of excitement in his chest. One, two, three...now! He pulled the string line down hard over the buttress. A flurry of feathers and squawking filled the air. Hector held the line taut with an expert hand. The red hen sprawled and twisted, screeching her protests. But the other two birds had left her, vanished into the shadows of the jungle.

'Now I got my girl,' he said to Lily, winking.

She laughed at him. 'Is that how you catch girls?'

'Eh, no,' he grinned, watching her laugh. 'I think they catch me.'

'Well yeah, you got legs like a chicken.' Lily pointed at his knees.

'Shut up,' he said smiling at her. His legs weren't like Tevuan legs, but he was only thirteen. His grandfather said he had lots of time yet to catch up.

The hen cowered as Hector knelt to pick it up. He tucked it gently under his arm and was about to stand up when an unusual shape caught his eye. He poked at the soil where the snare had been. 'What's this?' he said, unearthing a long metal object.

'A bit of iron,' said Lily.

Hector stood up and wiped it against the tree buttress to clear off the leaf litter, then turned it to catch the light. 'It's shiny. Well, not that rusty anyway.'

'Maybe it's a bush knife.'

'No, it's too long,' he said. He guessed it was as long as a softball bat, probably longer. 'No, I think it's…it's a sword.'

'A sword? Show me?' Lily pulled at his shoulder, trying to get a better look. The chicken squawked then settled again in Hector's armpit. 'It can't be a sword, there's no handle.'

'The grip must have rotted away, but there's still the metal underneath,' Hector muttered. He looked at the narrow flat end where once there would have been leather strapping. There was a hole, and inscriptions etched down the side. 'This is all that's left of the hilt and see—Japanese writing.' He tilted the blade and peered at the writing. 'The chicken must have dug it up. Do you think it's from the war?'

'What?' said Lily, frowning.

'Maybe it's from the war, you know, like the helmets and guns and things people sometimes find.'

'Don't be stupid. They didn't have swords.'

'Well how'd they cut people's heads off? With a karate chop?'

'*Suh!* I've never seen one before,' she said.

Hector held it gingerly, as if he feared it would leap up and cut off his own head.

'So what *have* you seen?' he asked, thinking of the keepsakes his grandfather had stored away: cartridges, a revolver and an old helmet. He also remembered the bomb that was unearthed near the primary school. He knew if you looked hard enough, there were World War Two relics everywhere on the island, just under the dirt beneath your feet.

'I don't think I've seen anything,' she said.

'Have you seen the beer bottles they used to drink from?'

'No. Where?'

Hector thought she sounded impressed. 'Up at the bunker on the cliff at Baringa Bay.'

'When did you go up there?'

'In grade six, the teacher took our class up. I've been there a few times since.'

'What's up there?'

'Just a bunker and a bath,' he said, grinning at her.

'A bath—bullshit!'

'True, I'll take you one day,' he said. He held the blade up once more, admiring its curve. 'It's like new, it's beautiful.'

'I like it,' Lily said.

With those three words she'd evoked the local custom of *pabwa*. Three small words which obliged every Tevuan to pass on a possession to whoever admired it. He had to give it to her now. Without hesitation he handed her the sword.

'It's heavier than I thought,' she said. 'And it's cold, so cold...'

He watched her face as she held the sword. She smiled to herself, and Hector thought he saw her nod her head ever so slightly.

'What are you going to do with it?'

'Keep it,' she said. 'I need it for something.'

Hector frowned. The sword would have been a great item to take home for his grandfather's collection. What was Lily going to use it for? Chopping firewood? Never mind, he was sure he'd find other treasures on his trips through the forest. He bound the chicken's legs together then pushed the remaining string into his pocket.

'We'll go up to the houses now and see what else we can find,' he said.

They picked their way through the forest, turning left at the small path which led up to Government Settlement. The first house they came to, a pale green bungalow surrounded by a low stone wall, was shaded by bean trees.

'Whose house is this?' Lily asked.

'Some white guy who lives on his own.' Cradling the chicken with difficulty, Hector climbed up onto the wall and beckoned Lily to follow. Her hesitation puzzled him. 'What's wrong?'

'Someone's there, I know it. I feel like the house is watching us.'

'Don't worry; there's no one around at this time of day. He'll be at work. Come on.'

Lily hoisted herself onto the terrace using the sword to support her, and they crept around the outside of the house. They'd find something lying about, Hector thought. If not, there was always the wash house. People often left things behind in laundries: clothes, soap, plugs.

If nothing else, you could always find pegs. As they rounded the front of the bungalow, the noise of an approaching car made them both duck.

'Shit, Hector, police!' Lily cried and she sped off around the back of the house.

Hector swore to himself. Her fleeing would only draw attention to them. He peered over the top of the wall. Sure enough, there was a police car and it had slowed out the front of the house. He heard the car doors opening and the engine die all at once. Hector turned and sprinted around the back. Lily beckoned to him from the wash house door.

As he reached the building he thudded against the half-closed door, and had to use both hands to force it open further. The chicken dropped to the ground and Hector stumbled over it. The bird squawked loudly and flapped about, struggling to free itself from its hobbles.

'Shut it up!' Lily hissed at him. 'They'll be on to us now, you idiot!'

two

Anbwido District
30 August 1942

On his way back from the leper camp Tepu saw Edouwe walking along the road towards him. Over her shoulders she carried a bunch of dry coconuts. Her smile broadened as he approached. Custom forbade them to talk openly without a chaperone, so she greeted him shyly.

'You must get back to camp, Edouwe. It's not safe on the roads with those devils on the island.'

'Thank you,' she nodded as they drew together. 'But they won't harm us, Tepu. The clinic doctor says the Japanese are frightened of lepers. They won't come anywhere near our camp.'

Tepu hoped she was right. She looked so confident; he envied her serenity. He didn't trust them, not one bit. 'Please promise me you'll be careful,' he pleaded.

'Be on your way, Tepu. We've talked too long here.' She lowered her gaze then moved on, leaving him staring after her, at the curves of her calf muscles and the sway of her hips.

When she was out of sight Tepu turned and made for Anbwido. It was a small settlement to the west of the leper colony where a few Tevuans had made their home. One family had been generous enough to give Tepu's family some land in exchange for labouring work his father had done. Now that his father had died, Tepu felt they were living on borrowed land and that they didn't have a real home.

Like many Gilbertese, Tepu's family had come to Tevua to find work mining for phosphate. He'd forgotten almost everything of his life in the Gilberts, everything except the gifts from his grandfather: the black stone and a few words about magic.

'You are a young shaman, boy. One day you'll know the strength of the ancient magic,' the old man had said to him. 'If you have courage and wisdom, you will use it well. If you are selfish and fearful it will poison your mind.'

He often wondered what his grandfather had meant. He knew the magic had something to do with the stone. He knew that some Gilbertese men had extraordinary powers and incredible strength, but the mystery of it all was never passed down to him. And now his family was fragmented and lost, there was no one he could ask to teach him these mysteries.

Laughter from the back of the house roused Christina from her book. There were people out in the yard. Were they the thieves her father had warned her about? She stiffened, listening to them talk in a language so alien to her own.

She eased herself up from the couch and crept into the kitchen. Parting the curtains carefully, she looked down to the terrace. Streaks of black filth bled from each block of stone that formed the low wall. Christina guessed it had once been whitewashed and smooth, but now years of neglect and tropical rain had worn away at the structure, crumbling and dissolving it until the tangled jungle beyond would eventually devour it.

Bodies were moving through the scrub on the other side. Christina could see the tops of their heads, the black sheen of their hair as they passed. Two figures snooping around, probably casing the place. Dad had said they often struck during the day, when no one was at home. She bit at her fingernails.

She'd already spent the first five days of her three-week holiday hiding away inside. Soon she'd be flying back to Melbourne and all she'd done was read novels, watch DVDs, and try to smile when her father's colleagues had dropped by for a drink, or they'd all gone out for dinner at the casino. Some holiday! Too many boring middle-aged men. She wished she were back in Mansfield, out horse-riding or paddock-bashing on her Mum's block.

Even chopping wood in freezing temperatures was preferable to sitting inside all day.

Suddenly one of the figures, a boy, clambered onto the wall. He held a live chicken under one arm and called out to his companion, who joined him a moment later. She looked a few years older than him, heavier and not as agile. Christina noted her hair, raven black and pulled into a tight ponytail. Like the other islander women she had seen, this girl looked proud but there was something fierce about her, something about her manner that frightened Christina. And the strangest thing about the girl was that she carried a long blade, like a sword.

The girl jumped down onto the terrace and looked about furtively.

Christina shrank away from the window. She watched the pair walk down the length of the house but lost sight of them as they turned the corner. Who were they, just kids wandering around taking a shortcut, or were they really up to something bad?

She heard a car approach, then the sound of it idling. It was too early for Dad to be home. Were these the accomplice thieves coming in cars to clean out the big things like the DVD player and the microwave? She ran to the front room and looked out. It was a police car, different from those in Australia, but unmistakably a police car with its blue lights on the roof. Christina froze. At the same time she heard someone running round the back.

She raced back to the kitchen window and pulled the curtain aside. The girl was fleeing along the terrace and in her fear she looked up at the window. It was only a moment, but Christina knew she'd been seen. She also knew that the girl's expression was more than fear. It was a warning: don't tell the police or you're dead, white girl! Without thinking, Christina signalled at her to head for the laundry.

Footsteps on the front porch brought Christina's attention back to the police. Their knock was tentative. She took a deep breath and walked to the door. Two overweight uniformed figures greeted her.

'Please excuse us, Miss,' the older one began, wiping sweat from his brow with a flick of his forefinger. 'We're looking for a boy and girl. We see them here, just now, in your yard,' he said, smiling.

'Yes, yes,' Christina's voice was squeaky. 'I saw them too. They ran down the path at the back. They ran into the forest. I saw them,' she lied.

The older one looked almost pleased to have missed his quarry and Christina could imagine why. She envisaged him toddling down the hill, sweat spilling from his forehead, his bulging stomach wobbling as he ran.

'Yes, down the hill, into the forest. There's a track down there, you know.'

The two officers exchanged glances, mumbled their thanks to Christina, then walked back up the path to their patrol car.

She shut the door behind them and waited. After a few moments they drove off and Christina felt her shoulders drop with relief. She could breathe properly again.

Should she go out to the laundry and see if the girl was

there? Perhaps she'd snuck away when the police were at the front door. She took a deep breath and walked down the kitchen steps onto the terrace.

The laundry stood away from the house at the edge of the yard. It reminded her of a ticketing booth or a food vendor's box at a country show. The big open windows were extensions of the concrete bench and wash trough. The door was ajar.

'Hello,' she called meekly. 'Hello, you can come out now. The police have gone.'

Silence. The girl must have slipped away. Christina pushed the door open.

'Ye-oow!' The squeal came as the door bumped against a body. She saw the boy and girl crouched on the floor. The girl was huddled awkwardly under the bench. The boy, still clutching his captive chicken, rubbed at his foot and swore.

'I'm sorry! I've hurt you. I didn't mean...' Christina spluttered.

'You stupid arse—what a dumb place to sit down!' shrieked the girl.

'*Suh*, shut up, you witch! You look stupid, all twisted up like the plumbing.' The two of them burst out laughing.

Christina felt embarrassed; they were ignoring her with their laughter and shouting. 'I'm sorry. I thought you'd be safe here. The police have gone,' she said, louder this time.

'And why'd they come? Did you tell them we were here?' the boy snapped.

'No!' she said, staring at him, noting his features for the first time. His left eye was disfigured by a huge scar that ran down onto his cheek. It made his face appear lopsided. Thick black hair grew long over his brow, probably to hide the scar, she thought. 'How could I tell them? You showed up the same time they did,' she retorted.

'What did you say to them?' the girl asked as she crawled out from under the bench.

Christina related her brief conversation with the police.

'Don't worry, they won't come back,' said the boy. 'They're too fat and lazy.'

'I want to know who called them,' the girl said.

'Must have been the Chinese,' the boy mumbled.

'What have you done to have the police after you?' Christina asked.

'Nothing, we did nothing,' the girl said, and her expression warned Christina not to pry further. The three of them looked at one another uneasily.

Finally the boy spoke. 'What's your name?'

'Christina Lowry. My dad works for the Lands Department. I'm here on school holidays, to spend time with Dad.'

'Where's your mother?' the girl asked.

'She's in Australia…my parents are divorced.'

The girl nodded. She kept staring at Christina's belly. Her gaze was unsettling. Hadn't she seen a navel ring before?

'I'm Hector, that's Lily,' said the boy. 'We're on holidays too, exploring the forest.'

'You talk shit, Hector,' Lily laughed.

Christina grinned. It was obvious that Hector was used to telling tales. He smiled back at her and she relaxed. He was the first islander she'd met who had actually been friendly, in an offhand sort of way. Even the few times she'd been out, hardly any locals had spoken to her; and if they did, it seemed rude, the way they never really looked you in the eye. And they didn't smile much, not like those friendly faces you see in travel brochures.

'Do you want a drink or something?' she asked. 'I could get you some water.'

'Yes, water,' Hector said, and they followed Christina out into the sunshine on the terrace. Hector still hugged the chicken and Lily dragged the sword.

Christina eyed it suspiciously. 'Where did you get the sword?' she asked.

Lily nodded towards the forest. 'Down there.'

'We think it's from the war,' Hector said. 'It's got Japanese writing on it.'

'Well it probably is. Dad says people are always finding World War Two artefacts on their land—unexploded bombs and things. I bet it's pretty valuable.'

'It's mine,' Lily pronounced, looking at her defiantly.

Christina was startled by her tone. 'I didn't mean I wanted to buy it or anything,' she said. 'It's just unreal to be surrounded by all these old things from the war.'

Lily rolled her eyes. 'It's just our shit of an island, nothing special.'

'Have you seen the pillboxes? There's one near Lily's house,' Hector offered.

'What...those concrete bunker things?

Hector nodded.

'Yeah, Dad told me the Japanese used to sit in them with their guns and look out for American ships. I've only seen them from the road.'

'They're not that great, Hector,' Lily said. 'Anything left there from the war was taken ages ago. People just get pissed on them now.'

'Still, Christina might like to visit one—tourism on Tevua!' he said, turning to the Australian.

'Why so friendly, Hector? Catching girls again, hey?' said Lily.

Christina smiled. Exploring a pillbox with these two would be better than lying on the couch all day watching the same old DVDs. At least she'd get some stories to tell her friends back in Mansfield.

'How about tomorrow?' he asked.

'Sounds good,' she said.

'After lunch then,' he said, checking that Lily agreed.

Lily raised her eyebrows. She was busy drilling holes in the terrace floor with the point of the sword.

'You're not going to bring that sword, are you?' Christina said.

Lily snorted. 'Nah, I'm going to hide it, until I need to use it,' she said coldly, staring at the blade.

Christina knew she wasn't bluffing.

three

Tepu had only enough time to snatch a cooking pot and a knife before the marines entered his home. He fled into the forest behind his younger brother, Tarema, who was pulling their mother along behind him. She objected to leaving the house and wailed in fear. Tepu caught up with them and tried to silence her.

'They'll hear you and know exactly where we are,' he hissed. But the marines had given up the chase. Their shouts and laughter rang through the forest and it made Tepu seethe.

'We'll make for Yamek,' he said, knowing that some families had fled to the weather coast of the island already. It was an inhospitable place to the northeast of Tevua where the wind howled, the soil was poor and the water brackish, but its rocky outcrops and pinnacles offered some protection from the invaders. Also it was still within an hour's walk of Baringa Bay and the leper camp, and

Tepu didn't want to be separated from Edouwe and her grandparents.

Once they reached Yamek they set up camp amongst the coral pinnacles, using them as corner posts for their new home: a crude lean-to. Over the next few days Tepu used his knife to cut coconut leaves for a makeshift roof. Tarema searched the forest's edge for firewood, and their mother gathered what seedpods and crabs she could find from the mangroves that grew in the salty ponds. Their nights were spent in quiet conversation, each of them consumed by fear and uncertainty.

'We'll go back and get some of our things, Mother,' Tepu said. It upset him to see her so withdrawn and dejected.

'You must be careful. They will eat you up if they catch you. They'll eat the whole island soon enough and dance on our withered souls.'

Tepu reassured her and he and Tarema set out the next morning at dawn. Once on the outskirts of Anbwido they crept back to the house. Tepu was shocked by what he saw—half the building was missing, the timber had been stripped away and only a small section of the frame remained. The roof had sagged to the ground. All their possessions were gone: no mats, no clothes, no kitchenware. Everything taken.

Tarema shook in an effort to suppress his tears, but Tepu stood tall and proud and would not cry even though the injustice made his throat prickle. He walked to the corner where his belongings had been. Only the smooth black stone lay in the sand, overlooked by the marines. Tepu knelt to pick it up and turned it over in his hands. He felt a surge of warmth, as if the stone had come alive all of a sudden.

He remembered the night his grandfather had given him the stone. The old man smelled strongly of coconut oil and sweat. His silver hair contrasted sharply against the red-brown skin of his face. 'This is the black stone of our ancestors, the black terns of the sea,' he said. 'A shaman has the stone to make himself strong and to use the ancestors' magic.'

Tepu was awestruck at the thought. He knew shamans were powerful and spoke to the spirit world. Each knew the laws and myths of their islands and the power of the gods.

'To be a shaman, when you reach manhood you must pass tests of strength and endurance,' he said. 'I am too old to come with you and guide you, Tepu. Keep this stone safe. It shall be a channel for my knowledge.'

But for many years the stone had lain neglected by Tepu in favour of fishing and exploring. Right now, however, amidst this devastation, its hidden magic called to him. If only he knew how to harness the power of his ancestors. I will discover it, he vowed to himself. I will learn this stone's magic and wield it against our enemies.

Lorelei Fasiti sat in the gaming room of the casino, her eyes reflecting the coloured lights of the screen in front of her. She chose her cards, a pair of kings, and pressed 'DEAL'. The digital cards flashed before her. No luck. The kings blinked back at her and she pressed 'DEAL' again.

'You winning anything yet?'

She didn't look up from the screen. She knew it was Daphne. 'No, nothing, bad luck day.'

'I got 200 dollars on this machine last week. Got a royal flush.'

Lorelei turned to look at her. Daphne was the child of a mixed marriage and Lorelei envied her almond eyes, as well as her ability to make light of everything. She'd always been like that, even when they were friends at school. Those easy days had gone, but their friendship had remained steady. 'Only 200? You should have bet more money.'

'I know, I'm gutless,' Daphne said, laughing.

'Finished all your money?' Lorelei asked her friend.

'Yeah, I've had enough. Besides, Olaf will kill me if I stay here all day. We're going out tonight.'

Lorelei smirked. Lucky bitch, she thought. Daphne's marriage still had some energy to it. She couldn't remember the last time she and Amos went out together peacefully. They couldn't play that game anymore. The sharp remarks they threw at one another had severed any affection they once had. The faithful husband—whatever happened to that concept? Daphne must have noticed the wistful look on Lorelei's face.

'You ought to check out if there's anyone in the bar,' Daphne said, lighting a cigarette. 'Never know, might find yourself a good one.'

'*Suh!*' she scoffed, eyeing Daphne with a straight face. Her upper lip curled. 'I'm not that kind of girl.'

Daphne slapped her on the back and the two of them burst into a fit of laughter.

'Eh, don't look now, girl. Here comes a good one. I've always liked a man in uniform, myself.'

Lorelei turned to follow Daphne's glance. Two police officers were approaching. Lorelei recognised them at once. The shorter man was her husband's old friend, Martin; his taller partner was the island's champion dart thrower.

'How's the winnings, Lorelei? Have you won enough to buy us a drink?' Martin joked. The two of them sat alongside her. Lorelei and Daphne exchanged bemused glances.

'I'll get some drinks,' Daphne said, and she waddled off to the bar.

'Cola, please, we're on duty!'

Lorelei continued with her game, trying her best to appear sober. Her eyesight swam a little each time the cards flashed on the screen. Pissed already and it was only early afternoon. God, what am I doing, she thought, just topping up after last night's binge? And what do these guys want, embarrassing me by sitting here?

'Saw your girl Lily today,' Martin said quietly.

'Yeah, so what?'

'She's been hanging round Government Settlement—in with bad company.'

Lorelei narrowed her eyes but continued to look at the screen. 'Who?'

'Hector Anisi.'

'That skinny kid with the busted face?'

Martin laughed. 'Yeah, that's him. They didn't pay for their meal at Lotus Restaurant either.'

'So what? Heaps of people rip off the Chinese if they can.'

Martin looked apologetic. He was not keen on enforcing the law. 'Well, I think she needs a warning.'

'OK. What about Hector?'

'We'll catch him one day,' Martin said with forced assurance.

Lorelei knew what that meant. They'd never bother to catch him, nor tell his family to issue a warning. Still it was understandable. There was only the grandfather with him: a strange old man who seldom spoke to anyone and spent days at a time wandering through the forest mumbling and shouting. No wonder the child was a delinquent. No one to keep him under control.

Daphne returned with the drinks and the conversation reverted to trivial things. After ten minutes of jokes and chatting, the policemen excused themselves.

'What was that all about?' Daphne said.

'Lil,' Lorelei sighed and turned to her friend. 'Give me a cigarette.'

'Sure, is she OK?'

Lorelei nodded, took a cigarette and leant towards the flame Daphne offered. She pulled on the cigarette heavily until it lit, then turned her attention back to the gaming machine. 'She's becoming a *trut* lately,' Lorelei mumbled.

'What's she done?'

Lorelei repeated Martin's story.

Daphne shook her head. 'That Hector kid is bad news; so is the grandfather, Riki. I heard he didn't even talk to his wife when she was alive. Crazy old bastard. But he can talk though. He'll tell you to bugger off if you get in his way.'

'The stupid *trut*, why doesn't she stay at home?' Lorelei spat. She stared blankly at her friend, but her breath came in small snorts of anger.

'What are you going to do? You look like you're going to kill her,' Daphne said.

'I'm just worried about her, that's all. She's getting so rebellious. She's been skipping school a lot too. Now it's the holidays, I can't keep her at home. I thought maybe she'd be easier to deal with than her brothers.'

'Well she *is* sixteen, isn't she?'

'Nearly.'

'I thought she hung around with your niece, Decima.'

'She normally does, but now Eide's diabetes is so bad, Decima's spending a lot of time nursing her. They're at the hospital a lot.'

'It's no good your sister's so sick,' Daphne mumbled. 'What's the latest news?'

'They've sent her home again, but she goes back for

dialysis every few days. I cook some meals for the kids, but the older ones can take care of themselves. We're doing what we can,' Lorelei said, trying to hide her concern.

'I suppose Lily feels left out,' Daphne said.

'No, it started before Eide's sickness got worse.'

'Don't worry. All teenagers are crazy. Just look at my kids.'

Lorelei smirked. Daphne's kids didn't seem bad. In fact they were just the opposite. She hardly ever saw Daphne's five kids roaming the streets at night. But then they lived at Praru, over the other side of the island. And their Samoan grandmother probably kept them at home with the threat of a big stick.

Still, she reasoned, what she saw in Anbwido every night was true of most of the island: groups of teenagers and kids as young as eight, gathered outside Chinese restaurants, nightclubs and the pool halls—little gangs with foul mouths, riding on bicycles, searching for mischief and something to steal.

She sucked hard on her cigarette and the curtain of smoke stung her eyes. 'I don't know, Daph, it's just that lately…I can't seem to connect with her. She won't do anything I tell her anymore. It shits me so much.'

Daphne raised her eyebrows in agreement.

Lorelei thought back to her youth, when she was too frightened to step out of line for fear of a beating. Something had been lost. The kids weren't scared anymore, not the way she'd once been.

Her friend laughed. 'I know, my girls are the same. All

you can do is lock them up and keep watching them, otherwise they'll be pregnant before you know it.'

'She's been so good at home for so long. Now though, she seems to want to run off all the time. I do everything I can to look after her, you know…'

'Well they're like that, aren't they?'

'She's got a room of her own and we've always been there for her and the boys, you know, a happy family.' Lorelei stopped suddenly, realising the lie she'd just uttered. 'If you could call it that,' she added in a whisper.

Who was she fooling? She was telling Daphne all this just to make herself look better in Daphne's eyes. She hadn't really been there for the family the last few years. She'd spent too much time at bingo or the casino, too much time so pissed she could hardly stand up. She knew it but she couldn't say it, not to her friends and not even to herself. It was a failing that she kept denying. She hated herself for feeling so weak.

Lorelei truly loved her kids, all three of them: Rongo, Lily and Cyrus. Even though Lil had been the toughest one of all to love. She had tried her best to accept Lily, and most of the time she could ignore the bad memories. When she remembered the good times with her daughter she smiled to herself.

Lil had been an inquisitive little girl sitting on her lap, with huge brown eyes in a round face. So much had changed in just ten years.

'Why do they hate us so much, Daph, after all we do for them?'

Daphne stubbed out her cigarette. 'I don't know, I just

don't,' she sighed and looked at her friend. 'But you can't hate them.'

Lorelei's top lip curled into a sneer. 'I'll have to go and teach her a lesson.'

four

By noon the Japanese had rounded up all able-bodied men and youths and told them, at gunpoint, that they had to work. An officer stood before them, sweating in his trim buttoned coat and gleaming black boots. He smiled with poorly disguised contempt at the assembled group of men. Through the aid of an interpreter who used halting broken English, he reassured them that in return for their labour they would be given weekly food rations. They would work for the glory of the Emperor, for Japan's victory in the Pacific. Tepu knew then that the Japanese were planning to stay on Tevua for a long time.

The invaders were small thin men but Tepu had learnt to fear them. It wasn't just because of the guns and swords they carried, but the way they beat people. They were unpredictable.

When the marines selected their work gangs, Tepu stiffened as he bowed, expecting a blow to the head, but none came. They pushed him forward and made him stand to one side with a group of stocky Tevuan men. Tepu looked on as the next youth in the line was considered. The boy's bowed head of black curls glistened in the sun, a model of subservience; but still the inspecting soldier slapped him. Tepu thought perhaps it was the relaxed curve of the boy's shoulder muscles that had invited the attack. He made a mental note always to appear frightened.

Tepu was the youngest member of his group. There were twenty of them altogether, many of whom he knew as acquaintances. They were assigned to clear the forest to the south of the island, not far from what had until recently been his village. Eight other men in his gang also camped out at Yamek. In the late afternoons they were escorted most of the way home: through the remains of Anbwido, past the leper camp, along the broad expanse of Baringa Bay to the hill that overlooked the windswept coast of Yamek. This suited Tepu well because as they marched he could look out for Edouwe and her grandparents.

In the evening of his first day of work he caught sight of her amongst the huts. Her jaw dropped in shock when she recognised him. He signalled to her discreetly, trying to convince her not to fear for him. But he saw the sorrow in her face as she shrank back into the shadows.

'Stand proud, my Gilbertese boy!' she called out from the safety of the huts.

One of the marines turned and levelled his gun at the camp. He shouted something menacing in Japanese but, seeing no one, he turned back to the work gang and screamed at them to walk faster.

Tepu's heart danced with happiness. It was dangerous for Edouwe to communicate with him, not only because of the Japanese threat but also because of local customs. But now she'd declared openly that he was *her* boy. It brought a smile to his lips and unconsciously he *did* stand taller, elated by her words. He'd have to keep in contact with her somehow. He needed to work out a plan.

Anbwido
Friday 25 June 2004

Inside her room, Lily took off her T-shirt. The singlet top she was wearing underneath smelled strongly of sweat, but she had nothing clean to wear. She hadn't done the washing yet. Should have done it today, she thought, instead of running around in the bush after chickens.

The sword was hidden under her mattress. A last resort if Eldon comes creeping in again, she resolved—but would she really use it? She didn't want to think about that. She just wanted it there for safety. It made her feel strong.

As soon as she'd taken it from Hector she felt a surge of power, a tingling rush of inner strength flowed up her arm. She knew the sword was special and she didn't want anyone else to have it. When Christina showed interest in the sword Lily knew she had to defend it, keep it safe. Something deep within willed her to say the sword was hers. She knew she shouldn't have spoken to Christina like that, but she couldn't help it.

She opened the wooden chest at the end of her room. Her whole world resided in that chest. There were T-shirts, shorts, a range of hair ties, her few cassette tapes, and her small blue box. She took out the box and opened it carefully. Inside was her collection: a piece of twisted coral, a plastic doll's hand and some wedding ring advertisements cut from magazines. She liked hands, other people's hands. When she thought of her own she was dispirited. Her left hand was so ugly and she couldn't hide it because she was left-handed.

She wished her skin were darker so no one could see the stain—the purple hue would not be so obvious then—but no, she was cursed with a lighter shade of brown. It made the birthmark vivid. Stupid boys said dumb things about her and blood and her periods. As if they'd know, the dumb shits. She had learnt to hurt them when she caught them, but she was getting heavier and she didn't run as fast as the little kids anymore. Now she just scowled at them and remembered their faces. They could wait. When they weren't expecting it she would hurt them. The little bastards. She'd teach them.

Lily replaced the blue box and shut the chest. She held her hands up in front of her and wondered what Jonah thought of her birthmark. Framed against the window, with the sunset behind them, the purple stain seemed to glow. Someone so perfect looking, like him, probably thought it was ugly.

Jonah was so hot, she often wondered why he ever bothered speaking to her at school. There were so many girls on the island who were gorgeous. She knew she didn't compare with any of them. If only she could gauge his interest in her. If only she could see him over these holidays, then maybe they could meet somewhere and then she'd know. She'd know if dreaming about him was a waste of time or not.

'Lil, where you been girl?' Lorelei's voice snapped.

Through her purple fingers, Lily saw her mother filling the doorway. She was a mass of breast and stomach, heavy and sticky with sweat, blocking Lily's only exit.

Lorelei wiped at her face with a tea-towel, smearing the sweat on her top lip—that fat upper lip, curled into a permanent sneer.

Lily looked down at the floor. 'I was out.'

'Out, always out!'

The doorway shook as Lorelei forced herself into the room. Lily covered her face with her arms, waiting for the blow. But it didn't come, not yet. Instead she felt her mother's fat fingers hook through her hair and tug.

'Where'd you go, why'd you run off?'

'Get away from you, yeah,' she whispered. But Lorelei didn't seem to hear anything now. Her tirade had begun.

'I heard you were in Government Settlement, running with that thief.'

'So what!'

'So I don't like it.'

'You don't like anything I do. It's alright for you to go off all day and all night.' That's when it came.

Bwack! Across the side of her head. It sent Lily spinning to one side, but Lorelei still held her by the hair.

She was as helpless as Hector's chicken.

'What do you mean?'

'You go off all the time!' Lily yelled, trying to wrench her mother's fingers off. The stench of beer and cigarettes hit her in the face as Lorelei screamed.

'You shut your mouth, girl.' Bwack! Against her jaw this time.

Lily stumbled but was held captive by her hair. She tried to squirm her way free, 'Man! You...'

'You shut up girl! You don't go sneakin' round Government Settlement. You don't go round with that thief.' The next blow hit her across the eyes. Darkness followed and she fell to the lino.

'*Trut!*' she heard her mother say. The doorway rattled as Lorelei left the room.

Lily's eyes burned with tears as she fought to open them. It took a moment for the blur of light to clear, then she focused on the upturned lino edge, blackened with filth and dust, and just out of reach, her mattress where the sword lay underneath.

'Some help you are,' she whispered.

That night Lily woke to find the rain had come. Her feet were getting wet. A cool breeze carried the rain in through the open louvres. She stood up and lurched to the side. Unsure of her balance, she leant against the wall. Her eyes were puffy and her head throbbed. She moved her mattress out of the wet patch on the floor, exposing the sword. Its blade glinted at her in the pale light.

She picked up the sword. It felt colder and heavier

than before. Where could she hide it? Perhaps inside the wooden chest? But it didn't lock. If anyone wanted to snoop inside they'd see it straight away. She decided to slip it behind the chest instead. It fitted easily. Satisfied, she went to shut the louvres.

Outside, bathed in the glow of the security light, a figure caught her eye. There was someone out there. Lily drew in her breath sharply and flattened herself against her door. She knew what to do: don't make a noise, don't ever let them know you're inside. Don't ever talk to anyone prowling around.

She struggled to breathe silently; her chest was tight with adrenaline and she thought she'd choke. She peeked through the louvres and saw the figure again, a Chinaman standing in the rain. He didn't seem to see her. He just stood there. If it wasn't for the rain, she'd swear he was saying something. His mouth and face were moving as if he was shouting, but no sound was coming out.

She turned away. Had he seen her? She couldn't be sure. She was getting wet standing beside the window, but she knew the screech and snap of shutting louvres would give her away.

Lily looked again. He was closer now, only a few metres away. She could feel her heart thumping and her face began to burn, but a chill had entered the room and she shivered as the rain spattered over her.

She was sure now that he was looking at her. She wanted to tear herself away from the window but found she couldn't move. He was mouthing something, shouting at her and all the veins and sinews in his neck strained.

His nostrils gaped and she saw hatred in his eyes. But he wasn't wet, even though he stood in the pouring rain.

Was she dreaming? Lily rubbed her eyes but the pain of her swollen face made her gasp. She couldn't be dreaming; the pain was real. Maybe that was it? Her eyes were so busted she was seeing things that weren't there.

'Who are you?' she stammered.

He continued his silent ravings.

Terrified, she held her breath. It had to be a ghost. She turned away from the window, knelt on the floor and fumbled for something to throw. Her rubber thong, yes that would do.

She stood up and confronted him. His black eyes bored into hers.

'Piss off, you *yani!*' She threw the thong at him and watched with relief as his image faded before her.

Lily slammed the louvres shut and crouched on her mattress, staring at the window. Her heart thumped and her whole body felt chilled. She shivered uncontrollably.

But the most unsettling sensation was in her left hand. The purple of her birthmark tingled hot as if she'd been stung by dozens of red ants. Had she slept on it awkwardly before the ghost materialised?

Would he come back? Why was a ghost hanging around here? So many thoughts and fears filled her mind, she thought she'd never sleep. But somehow sleep came to her as she sat with her back to the wall, wrapped in a sodden sheet in the far corner of her room.

As dawn approached Lily dreamt she was drowning, drowning in a sea of blood and tears. A rickety boat bobbed on the waves, out of reach. It was a familiar nightmare, where she plunged into the black waters of the ocean only to find them filled with blood, and where the wail of a crying woman pierced her dreams.

five

Mawendo District
3 December 1942

The mist of dust and coral shards cleared from the blast and the marines signalled Tepu's gang to clear the debris. The sun bit into his skin, sweat streamed from every pore of his body and his limbs ached. He longed to rest for a few minutes in the shade, but he dared not stop work. They were always watching, waiting for a man to stumble.

Torn coconut leaves strewn amongst the rubble of logs and rock were all that remained of the life-giving palms. Tepu's hatred of the Japanese grew with every fallen tree. *Our food destroyed for the sake of a runway*, he thought. *What would they eat? Aeroplanes?*

He bent to lift one end of a log and saw a cluster of green coconuts in the wreckage nearby. Immediately he became aware of his thirst, but he fought the desire to reach out for them. He picked up a broken coconut leaf and threw it over the nuts. If he was lucky he could smuggle them out with the next load. The thought gave him a surge of strength as he dragged his log from the rubble to the bonfire site.

Tepu heaved the log onto the pile. Sweat stung his eyes. He wiped a dusty arm across his brow and turned for the next load. Someone was shouting. He ran back towards the blast site.

He was too late. Another worker, an older Tevuan with a large family, had found the coconuts and tried to hide them at the edge of the forest. The man hadn't been careful enough: one of the marines had caught him and forced him to hand over the coconuts. Then the beating began, blow after blow with a large stick. The man bent and twisted beneath the punishment.

Attracted by the commotion, the nearest Lieutenant strode towards them, barking orders and drawing his sword.

The worker cowered beneath the blows. Tepu stared in horror as the Lieutenant closed in and the worker crumpled to the ground. But the Lieutenant didn't use his sword. He used his boot instead, and the smack of leather in the worker's face made Tepu wince. Don't fall down, he thought—if they beat you, you mustn't fall down.

All the men hated this Lieutenant. They learnt to recognise him from a distance. He was the same size as the others but he walked quickly, his long black boots flashing in the sunlight and his head jutting forward. His face was thin and flat and his empty black eyes showed no emotion.

The Tevuans called the Lieutenant 'Egirow'. It was their word for angry. Most officers ignored the Gilbertese and Tevuan workers, but not Egirow. He was always interfering with the marines he supervised, joining in with the beatings. Some even said he beat his own marines.

The Japanese were increasingly suspicious of any communication between the islanders. Each morning and evening when Tepu marched past the leper colony he looked out for Edouwe. He always positioned himself at the edge of the group so he could signal to her if he saw her. He would pretend to wipe sweat from his brow and Edouwe would look as though she was swatting an insect away. They both had to be careful not to attract the guards' attention. Sometimes the guards were so close it was impossible even to look at one another.

Most mornings Edouwe hid behind a cluster of coral pinnacles on the outskirts of the camp. If she couldn't be there she left a sign: a rock strategically placed on top of one of the pinnacles. In the evenings he often heard her whistle from the shadows of the huts. He dared not look around, but he knew it was Edouwe calling to him. Sometimes he saw her dart from one hut to another just as they passed and the sight of her lifted his spirits. But the daily sightings were not enough. Tepu longed to speak to her.

Barbecued fish and sausages and a huge mound of rice lay on the card table in front of them: Hector and his grandfather picked at the fish in turn, pulling the soft white flesh easily from the bones that were like toothpicks.

They sat on the porch looking out through the trees towards the sea. Soon the sun would be high in the sky. Between the trees and the ocean a stream of battered early model Landrovers, scooters, and rusted out sedans churned past.

'The Japs had swords, didn't they, Ibu?' Hector asked as he sucked the grease from his fingers.

The old man raised his eyebrows. 'They had swords.'

'We found one a few days ago,' Hector said as he picked up a portion of rice in his fingers.

The old man stopped chewing. His hand stopped in midair, poised above the rice. He stared at Hector. 'Where?'

The boy nodded to the right, indicating the scrub behind the house. 'Place I got the chicken.'

The old man coughed and his body heaved with each hacking bark. Finally, he composed himself and spat over the side of the balcony. Hector offered him a jug of water and a metal cup. The old man poured himself a drink, his large fingers fumbling with the lid as he tried to replace it. 'Where's the sword now?' he asked.

'Lil's got it.'

'I'd like to see it,' he whispered.

Hector knew he would. He was always interested in things from the war, old photos, legends and stories of long ago. 'I'll tell her. She didn't believe me when I said the Japs had swords.'

'Probably her family doesn't know much about the past. So much is lost. The young parents don't tell their children anything now. They don't guide them.' He looked steadily at Hector. The lines under his eyes made his expression sag. 'You're unlucky to have lost your parents, but you are blessed to have an *ibu* to teach you.'

Hector rolled his eyes. Blessed! Sometimes he thought he was cursed. Like when his grandfather decided to lecture him. He went on and on, telling the same old stories Hector had heard a thousand times before.

'It is a sad island, Hector. Before, we were proud people. Now we're just a land of drunks.'

'Yeah, yeah, yeah, I know, "don't come drinking beer round here",' Hector mimicked.

The old man leant back on his chair and scratched his bald head with both hands. The muscles in his arms sagged the same way his face did. Hector reckoned he would have been a strong man in his youth—not muscular, but wiry. Now his belly had thickened and his wrinkled face had the suppleness of rubber.

'Ibu, why did they chop people's heads off? You know, like you said they did to some men during the war.'

'Very cruel, the Japanese, Hector. Very cruel. They thought the men were spies for the Americans. They thought they told the Americans to bomb the runway. So, chop, chop.' He made a cutting gesture at his throat.

'Did you see it?'

'No, but others did.'

Hector swallowed hard. What if the sword they'd found had killed someone? The skin on his spine prickled. 'But why did they kill people and not just keep prisoners?'

The old man chewed on one of the charred sausages, taking his time to answer. 'They didn't kill everyone...I don't know, Hector. They did everything for their god. They had to win the war for their god.'

Hector knew of only one god. The one they'd been dragged along to church to worship every Thursday and Sunday. 'Who's their god?'

'The emperor.'

'What emperor?'

'He's like their king. They were so stupid. They thought he was a god, like Jesus maybe.' The old man turned the fish over to expose the uneaten side.

Hector was puzzled. 'But didn't they go to church? Was it so long ago we didn't have churches then?'

'*Suh!* They were not Christians.' The old man began to chuckle. 'And anyway, it wasn't long ago. How old do you think I am? One hundred?' He laughed at his little joke, coughed roughly then leant over the balcony and spat again.

'Well, when was the war, Ibu?'

'About sixty years ago.'

'So how old were you when they came?

'About the same age as you...fifteen I suppose, I don't know what year I was born.'

'I'm thirteen,' Hector said, secretly pleased that his *ibu* thought he was older.

'Well then, something like that.' The old man nodded.

Hector knew what five years, or even ten were like, but when people said sixty or one hundred it didn't mean much to him. 'So when did the churches come?'

'Oh before that, when the Germans came, maybe a hundred years ago or more. They brought Christian stories, their Lutheran church. Some Tevuans married Germans. Lots of German names, German words, German customs mixed with island ways. They stayed a long time, till World War One, then the British came.'

'OK, so before that, didn't we go to church?'

'No.'

'Did we know about Jesus?'

'No. Tevuans had stories about their own gods. And the Gilbertese had different gods: gods of the sea, the earth and the dead. The Gilbertese had ancestor spirits and the Tevuans had legends, like the girl in the moon. Both people knew of ghosts and witches and evil demons. You know those stories.'

Hector remembered all the ghost stories from when he was a child. He was still frightened by the story about the evil witch at Baringa who lured children away from their mothers, but he dared not admit it. Even though he felt the power of these old stories, he didn't know whether he should believe them or not. 'But are they real, Ibu, these ancestor spirits and ghosts?'

'They're real if you believe,' said the old man, 'and if you feel ancient magic in your blood then they are true and real like you and me.'

Hector grunted and cleared away the remains of their lunch. 'I don't know, I think I need to see a ghost first, before I believe,' he said. Should he dismiss the ancient magic as superstition or put his faith in it?

The old man looked at him with a tired expression. 'One day you will understand, Hector. You are about old enough.'

'What do you mean?'

'Some people feel these things as children and others as teenagers. Some with Gilbertese blood are shamans; they know the spirit world.'

Hector felt uneasy, as if a dark cloud had covered the sun. He shivered and changed the subject. 'I met an Australian yesterday, a girl. She's here on holidays.'

His grandfather smiled.

'I'm going to show her the pillbox down near Lily's house today.'

'You go with another girl, please.'

'Yes, I'm going with Lily,' Hector was irritated. Didn't his *ibu* know those old customs weren't important anymore? The old man grunted and began washing the dishes.

Hector said goodbye and left the house. Today had been a good day—his grandfather had felt like talking. Sometimes they would go weeks without his *ibu* saying a word. Hector was used to it, but no one else under-stood Riki's strange behaviour. People thought his *ibu* was crazy and their reactions annoyed Hector more and more. Why couldn't people just accept that the old man was different?

The track from Hector's hut was covered with potholes. He pedalled his bike expertly between them and took the turn that led downhill past where Lily's cousins lived. He saw figures on the *meneaba* beside the house. It was Lily and her cousin Decima.

'Where are you going?' Decima screeched.

He hit the brakes and skidded to a halt. Black slush from the track sprayed sideways. 'I was going to get Lil,' he said looking at Lily.

She turned away from his gaze.

'Remember, we said we'd take Christina to see the pillbox.'

'We'll go soon. Decima's coming too,' she muttered.

'Aren't you going to the hospital?' he asked Decima.

'Not today, Mum said she'll be fine for a while. So I'm free!' She grinned.

Hector got off his bike and propped it against the *meneaba*. The girls were sitting cross-legged, playing cards. He climbed up onto the platform with them. Lily didn't look too good. One side of her face was fat and her eye was dark and bloodshot. She must have had a fight last night.

'Want to play last card?' Decima asked. Her straight narrow features made her look serious, even when she was being friendly.

'Yeah, why not.'

Decima shuffled the cards and began dealing them. Lily sat in silence. Hector tried to catch her attention, but she avoided him.

'Hector, you know anything about ghosts round here in Anbwido?' Decima said.

'Ghosts, there are ghosts all over this island. That's what my grandfather says.'

'Riki! Riki!' Lily taunted him.

Hector blushed.

'*Suh!*' he spat at her, 'Shut up!' He grabbed her by the shoulder and pushed hard. Lily laughed and fell off the platform onto Hector's bike. She and the bike toppled to the ground, her feet tangling in the handlebars as she fell.

Hector couldn't help chuckling. She looked ridiculous lying beside the bike with her legs stuck in the air.

Lily glared up at him, her expression hard to read through the puffiness of her face, then she laughed again. Decima joined in, but ran to help her up.

'*Ngaitirre!* I'll get you for that,' Lily snapped.

'You couldn't catch me,' he said.

'Hey, sit down,' Decima said, gathering up the scattered cards. She sat down and began counting them.

Hector was enjoying this: two older girls giving him all this attention, talking to him like like a friend. What a way to spend the afternoon!

'What are these ghosts your *ibu* talks about?' Lily asked. 'Has he seen any?'

'Yeah, I think so. You know that story about the witch who calls for her children?'

'We're missing some cards,' Decima whined, but Hector and Lily weren't listening.

'Has he seen her?' said Lily.

'Well, he thinks he knows who she was. Says she was

an evil woman…lived at the edge of Anbwido and Baringa long ago. She ate babies.'

'Everyone knows that. What about men ghosts?'

Hector shrugged. 'Probably. He knows a lot about ghosts.'

'Come on you guys, help me look for these cards. Three are missing.'

'How come he knows so much?' asked Lily.

'Because he's Gilbertese. He knows about spirits and healing and things.'

'My family thinks he's weird,' Lily said.

Hector looked at her and his voice rose. 'He's not weird. He's just grumpy. He likes being alone.'

'Where is he now?' she asked.

'Home, but he's going out fishing soon, at high tide.'

Lily laughed at him, 'See, goes out in the hot sun, I told you he was weird.'

Something tightened in Hector's throat and he couldn't be sure if Lily was teasing him or not. 'Shut up. He's not weird.'

'We can't play cards, if the joker and two other cards are missing. Where are they?' Decima directed her gaze at Hector.

He looked hurt. 'Me, why do you think it's me?' He slipped a hand up the leg of his shorts and pulled out the missing cards. 'Is this what you want?'

'Bastard!' the girls screamed at him in unison.

The three of them whooped with laughter and Hector felt like a king.

'Come on, let's play,' Decima said. Her small dark hands flashed back and forth as she dealt the cards.

'Why do you want to know about ghosts?' Hector flicked a card onto the discard pile between them.

'Lily saw one the other night, didn't you?'

There was a long silence while Lily picked up a card. 'I think so,' she whispered.

'What was it like?' Hector asked. He was keen to hear an eyewitness report. If someone had really seen a ghost, then he was willing to believe it was true.

Lily told him what she'd seen. Hector's mind was immediately filled with ideas. 'We ought to see if he comes back—perhaps he was trying to tell you something. Who do you think it was?'

Lily looked at him with a pained expression. 'I don't know. I thought he was Chinese.'

Hector thrust a card on the discard pile and hissed his displeasure at the progress of the game. 'Do you think he's Japanese? A soldier from the war? Maybe he died somewhere in Anbwido.' He looked eagerly at Lily, hoping she'd feel the same excitement about it. Her face was sad, swollen and disfigured. She sniffed and looked at him, impassive.

'I didn't like it, Hector. It wasn't fun. It wasn't a game.'

Her tone made him feel uncomfortable, and willing to believe her. He wanted to be there at night, around her house, ready to see the ghost if it came back. But he knew he couldn't; that was the easiest way to get a real beating. If someone caught you hanging around their house at night, they'd be thinking all sorts of bad things. They'd think you were there to sweet-talk their daughters or rape them. They'd think you were hanging around ready to steal their DVD players and stereos or something. No, Lily's house at night was out-of-bounds. He'd just have to ask his grandfather what he knew.

An uncomfortable silence grew between them. Finally Decima spoke: 'We'd better go and get Christina.'

The three of them walked up the bush track that led to Government Settlement. At Christina's house they stood on the terrace, unsure of what to do. Decima thought they should knock on the door, not call out like they normally did at Tevuan homes. Hector plucked up the courage to approach the kitchen door. He tapped on it as if he thought it would break. The two girls doubled up laughing at him.

The door opened.

'Where have you been? It's nearly three o'clock. You said you'd be here after lunch,' Christina complained.

'That's island time,' Hector smiled.

'They don't have a watch,' Decima offered.

Christina glared at her. Hector stumbled through an introduction. 'Decima's Lily's cousin. She's been to Australia...she's our friend,' he said.

'Oh, well I'm glad you're here. I thought you'd forgotten me.' She glanced at Lily who had turned away and was already heading back to the path.

'Are these your new friends?' A man's voice came from a shadow in the doorway behind Christina.

'Yeah, Dad, this is Hector, and Decima, and Lily's over there,' she gestured. A tall man with a red face and a sharp nose followed Christina out the door. His arms were covered in small brown spots, like the belly of a fish. Hector could see the resemblance between the man and Christina, except the skin on Christina's arms wasn't so spotty.

'Nice to meet you,' the man said, wincing in the sun's glare. 'I'm Brett Lowry.' He reached out to shake Hector's hand.

Hector could smell the yeasty fragrance of beer on the man's breath.

'When will Christina be back?' Brett asked.

Hector was confused. How could he know when they'd be back? He couldn't see into the future.

'Don't stress, Dad,' Christina scowled.

'Before dark,' Decima reassured him, and they set off down the hill.

'Enjoy yourselves!' Brett called out after them.

Lily led the way down the track. She didn't turn back to join in the conversation. Hector assumed she was embarrassed about her face but Christina hadn't noticed. She seemed more interested in escaping from the house.

By the time they'd reached the Ring Road Hector had learnt that Christina was in Year Ten at school in country Victoria and loved horse-riding. Hector had never seen a real horse and couldn't stop asking questions.

Decima laughed at his efforts to be friendly. 'Do you want to steal a horse just like you steal a chicken?' she teased.

Lily was waiting for them to catch up. 'There's the pillbox.' She pointed to the other side of the road. Only the top of the dome was visible above the high grass and creeper around the base. Beyond the pillbox the reef stretched out to the sea.

They crossed the road and waded through the grass. Hector hauled himself onto the dome and the girls followed. There wasn't much room for the four of them, so he slid down onto the sand on the other side. The view out to sea was clear. Sometimes the haze on the horizon played tricks on his eyes, but today the sea was sharply defined: a dark blue against the bright sky.

Hector imagined what an American ship must have looked like all those years ago. 'They watched for ships all along the coast,' he said.

'It's a great view,' Christina said.

Lily rolled her eyes. 'It's not that great, same every day really.'

Decima had to agree with her. 'And these pillboxes always smell like piss.'

'At least you live near the sea. I hardly ever get near the ocean,' Christina said.

'What's it like where you're from?' Lily asked.

'There're a few hills around, but it's just a lot of grass. And half the year it's so dry that the grass is brown—same every day really, except when it snows in the mountains,' Christina said smiling at Lily.

'Snow! What's that like?' Hector said.

'Cold and wet.'

Lily grinned. 'I guess you think it stinks where you're from too?'

'It's OK, but I don't want to stay there forever.'

Lily pointed at Christina's midriff. 'Why do you have a ring through your belly button?' she asked.

Christina laughed. 'It's just fashion. It's cool, don't you think?'

'Tevuans aren't into it,' Decima said, spitting into the sand. 'Girls are supposed to cover up.'

'Oh, I didn't realise it offended people,' Christina said, blushing.

'Stuff them,' Decima said. 'Wear what you like. They'll get over it.'

'The Japs sat down here,' Hector interrupted. He pointed to a small opening that served as a door at the base of the pillbox.

Christina jumped down to inspect it. 'Wow. There's not much room inside. They must have been small soldiers, especially to get their guns and swords and everything in as well.' She ran her hand over the surface of the concrete. 'Dad said they made these pillboxes as soon as they invaded. '

'How come your dad's such an expert?' Decima said.

'Oh, he's right into the war and all that. He never shuts up; even raves on about it at breakfast.'

'Did you tell him about the sword?' Lily asked sharply.

Christina looked alarmed. 'No, I…I just asked him this morning if the Japanese killed many people and he told me about swords and guns and stuff.'

'Like what stuff?' Lily demanded.

'Well, only a few people in Japan made swords. The guy who made them put his name on the handle part before the grip went on. You know, like a brand.' Lily's stare was rattling Chritina. 'Yeah well that would be the Japanese writing on the sword you found, I guess. Dad said only the officers had swords. They were special. I don't really get it, but the officers had a kind of spiritual connection with their swords.'

'What do you mean?' Hector said.

'Well, their swords were like a part of them and they couldn't bear to be separated from them, not even when they died. So, if an officer died the Japanese sent the body home with his sword so he could be buried peacefully. Otherwise his spirit would be messed up.'

'What does that mean?' asked Decima.

'The spirit stays around and haunts the place where he died.'

'Do you mean like a ghost?' Hector looked directly at Lily. He could see she was afraid.

'I suppose so,' Christina said. 'But it can't be true. There's no such thing as ghosts.'

There was a long silence. Lily, Hector and Decima exchanged glances.

'I think we've seen enough here,' Decima said. 'Do you want to see more on Monday, Christina? I'm sure we could show you some other sights.' She and Lily slid off the pillbox onto the grass.

Hector scrambled back over the top of the dome. Christina hesitated. Hector saw she was confused. They'd only just got here and they were leaving again. She must have sensed the tension that Lily generated.

Should they tell her about the ghost? Then she might understand why her comments were too dismissive. But it was risky. She'd just think they were all superstitious idiots, dumb islanders.

No wonder most Tevuans felt ill at ease around white people. His *ibu* had told him that long ago the island had suffered under the British and the Australians. They'd treated the islanders badly, bossed them around and stolen half their money. Hector had forgotten if it was before the war or afterwards. Christina didn't seem bossy or stuck up, but it was best to be careful.

He watched Lily and Decima cross the road ahead of them. What if Christina's story was true—what if Lily had disturbed a ghost by taking the sword? Hector knew she'd have to return it. But he'd given it to her when she said she liked it. *Pabwa*. He couldn't ask for it back. And besides, Lily got so fierce whenever the sword was mentioned. He was certain she would never return it to the forest.

six

Mawendo District
18 December 1942

Tepu pushed a boulder to one side, paused and looked up. His eyes met Egirow's stare and in that instant he realised he'd been too slow to salute. In desperation he raised his hand. But the Lieutenant knocked Tepu's arm down, sneered at him and slapped him in the face. 'Stand up! Salute!'

Tepu lurched backwards, raising his hand to his head, but the motion lacked urgency. Egirow was furious. He brought his rifle butt down on the boy's head. Tepu rocked from the impact. Blood streamed from somewhere above his left eye. A second blow came, and a third, and through the searing pain Tepu held one thought clearly in his mind: keep standing. No matter how much it hurts, keep standing.

That night, cut, bruised and angry, Tepu took the black stone and walked into the forest. The marines rarely patrolled this part of Yamek, but he had to be vigilant all the same. Sometimes they moved about in the evenings, as silent as cats. If they caught him during the night-time curfew he would surely be beaten and he'd had enough beating for one day.

Tepu recalled his grandfather's words, 'You must pass tests of strength and endurance.' Was today's assault one of those tests? How many more would there be?

He made his way between coral pinnacles, over boggy ground and rotting logs until he found a secluded spot: a small clearing between three pinnacles at the base of a cliff. Taking his bearings he guessed he'd walked as far as Baringa District.

He took the black stone from his pocket and ran his fingers over the smooth surface. 'What is your magic?' he whispered, willing the stone to answer him. But the stone was silent. He placed it on the ground and looked up, pleading silently to the gods and his ancestors for help. The stars blinked back at him. Tepu sat for a long time, staring up at the universe. Eventually he gathered enough courage to speak aloud.

'Ancestors, hear me. Reveal your secrets,' he murmured. Again there was silence. This time he shut his eyes and repeated his plea, over and over until it became a chant, a low rumbling tune.

After a while, Tepu's limbs felt numb. He longed to rub them or stretch his legs, but he was determined to keep up his call to the spirit world. Just when the pain became unbearable he heard the flapping of seabirds overhead. They were black noddies, returning to their roosts from the ocean. Their chattering reassured Tepu—

he knew his chant was working because his grandfather's totem was the black noddy sea tern. He kept his eyes shut and concentrated on the image of the bird in his mind.

Soon Tepu felt as if his body had begun to float on air. Whispers surrounded him. He shivered. A flash of light entered his brain and subsided just as quickly. A low, rasping voice called to him from the darkness.

'Pick up the stone,' the voice said. 'The stone will guide you.'

Tentatively Tepu opened his eyes. He was surprised to find himself still sitting on the ground. The stone glowed before him with a green light. He picked it up, felt its warmth flow along his arm and overpower his fear. Confidence swelled within him. Tepu was certain now that the stone was meant for him. He felt an indescribable link, a sense of belonging, of trusting the stone and his inner self. They had become one. He sat motionless, clutching the stone to his chest until a movement above startled him.

Tepu looked up and saw the outline of a black sea tern perched on one of the pinnacles. It ruffled its feathers and gave a small whistle. Tepu knew it was his grandfather come to help him. Awestruck, he fell forward.

'Great and wise grandfather bird, I thank you,' he spluttered.

The bird's eyes shone with a green light. Its gaze drew Tepu to his feet, filling him with strength. He stretched out his arms towards the bird in reverence. The noddy whistled once more, spread its dark wings and vanished.

Tepu blinked. The darkness enveloped him with a sense of calm. He returned to his camp feeling both drained and elated. He'd made contact with the spirit world. Now he'd have to learn the ancient magic.

Leper Beach
Anbwido
Sunday 27 June 2004

Sausages bobbed up and down in a basin of water lying in the sand. Lily knelt and broke open the plastic wrapper on a polystyrene tray of chicken wings. She dropped most of the meat into the basin then eased the last few wings out of the packet. She knew it would all thaw quickly in the sun—just like her family. They'd all get drunk quickly in the sun, and start arguing with one another. She wished she didn't have to come along and witness it. Still it was a family barbecue, her dad's big day, thirty-nine and still going strong.

She watched her mother unpacking the old Landrover. Lorelei pulled out two folding chairs and wrenched each one open in turn. Stupid things, Lily thought. She remembered how her dad had sat in one once, how it stuck to his arse when he tried to get up. God they'd all laughed. Sometimes he was such a clown. Now he just looked pissed off with Lorelei. They'd already been arguing and it was only mid-morning.

'Come and get this fire organised,' she screamed at him. She was hauling bricks out of the back of the Landrover.

Amos grunted at her. He had placed two eskies on the edge of the clearing and was emptying bags of ice into them.

A car's engine revved from the track beyond the clearing. Lily turned to see an old white sedan park in the grass underneath the beach almonds. The rusty doors opened and her uncle Eldon emerged from the passenger seat. He ran his hands through his spiky hair and called out to Amos.

'Hey, birthday boy, you'd better get a beer into you before the party warms up.'

Lily felt sick when she saw Eldon. He was probably still drunk from the night before. He was always drunk and usually dragged Lily's older brother Rongo along with him. Rongo had just turned eighteen and thought it was cool to spend most of his time drinking, so he didn't mind. This time though, Eldon had hitched a ride with Joachim, their mutual drinking partner. Joachim, who was as fat as a wild boar, eased himself out of the driver's seat, then fumbled on the dashboard for a cigarette lighter.

'Did you get the tomato sauce and the tongs?' Lorelei shouted. 'That's what I told you to go back and get.' She waddled over towards the car, the hem of her *mu-mu* catching in the long grass.

Eldon lifted a slab of beer out of the back seat and balanced it expertly on one shoulder. He ignored his sister as he carried it past her, over to Amos and the eskies.

'What kind of sauce is that?' she shouted, following him.

'Don't worry,' he said waving at her dismissively, 'we

sent Rongo to get the sauce. Here, have a beer.'

Eldon ripped the edge off the carton and pulled out a can for her. She snatched it from him, ripped the ring-top off and threw it in the grass. After a long guzzle she wandered back to the Landrover and continued building the barbecue.

Lily looked down at the sausages. She hated these gatherings. Apart from Decima, there was never anyone to talk to. Why was she cursed with brothers and mostly male cousins? Every cousin on Amos's side of the family was a boy. It was better on her mum's side. Lorelei and Eldon had three sisters. One died young from hepatitis, but Eide, Decima's mum, and her sister Gertrude went on to have ten children between them. Auntie Gertrude lived in Tonga with her husband so Lily never saw them. But Auntie Eide had six children and number four was Decima. Numbers five and six were both girls and still at primary school, so they didn't hang around with Lily and Decima too much.

Decima was the only girl her age and, because Auntie Eide was sick, her family wouldn't be coming until later in the afternoon. By then everyone would be so pissed they wouldn't be able to talk without a fight erupting. Last time Rongo and one of her cousins were taken to hospital because they'd smashed beer bottles over each other. This time Lily wished someone would hit her uncle Eldon.

The sound of another vehicle disturbed her thoughts. Rongo lurched through the grass on Lorelei's scooter. A plastic bag containing the missing barbecue tongs hung from the handlebars. Behind Rongo another battered

Landrover entered the clearing. It was crammed full of Amos's relatives from the other side of the island. A good time to escape, Lily thought. She walked quickly to the track that led to Leper Beach.

Trees spread their branches as far as the water's edge. Coral pinnacles stood at both ends of the bay. They were like rocky columns that formed the sides of a giant window in the sand, no more than fifteen metres wide. The leafy canopy above formed the rest of the window.

Lily sat on the shore, digging her toes into the sand. The beach was in shadow. Even though it would soon be midday the air was cool and she shivered. She looked out at the calm waters rippling over the reef and tried to relax.

It was so hard. Every time she saw her uncle Eldon she was sick with shame and disgust. She didn't want to be anywhere near him, she didn't want him even to look at her.

She remembered the night it had happened as if time didn't count. The pain was so real it consumed her with hatred each time she saw him. Eldon had woken her, whispered to her to be quiet and pinned her down. The stink of beer and cigarettes had clogged every part of her. She had tried to jerk to the side.

'Don't move,' he'd snarled.

She'd struggled. 'Get off me,' she'd gasped, but that's all she'd said. He whacked her, just like Lorelei always did, where her lip was already split and tender. The scab burst, opening like a mango turned inside out. She'd felt the blood in her mouth and tasted it.

His hand pushed in between her legs and she'd wriggled to one side in a desperate attempt to get away, but there was only the wall. There was no escape.

Instinctively she had gone outside her body as she'd lain there—to float somewhere on the edge of the reef. There was an old wooden boat anchored a few metres out from the reef. She'd looked into the depths, the big blue-black emptiness that heaved and swelled, and felt herself sinking into the gloom. But the sensation of drowning had overcome her and she'd gasped for air as Eldon rolled off her.

Now here at Leper Beach tears hung in her eyes, threatening to spill down her cheeks, but she brushed them away. There was no one who could help her. She dared not tell even Decima. The shame would be too much. Be brave, she told herself. You mustn't cry. You must never cry, even when you fall down and you bleed, you mustn't cry.

Blood, why was she thinking of blood? It had been in her dreams again last night: her drowning, sinking in the blood-soaked sea. There had been wailing too and a whisper of it remained when she opened her eyes. Someone had been screaming with pain, crying out for help and there was nothing she could do because she was sinking into the depths and her purple hand burnt. It prickled unbearably when she woke.

Lily shuddered at the memory. Somehow she knew the vision in her mind belonged here, at Leper Beach. It was a mystery how such a nightmare originated from this tranquil place. She felt the beach was special and always came here whenever there were family barbecues at the clearing nearby. She tried to imagine who the lepers were and what happened to them.

The slapping of thongs along the path jolted her back to the present.

'What you doing down here girl? You've got work to do,' Lorelei said.

'Yeah, yeah, yeah, I'm coming.'

She wished she could just disappear. The stupid barbecue was all a farce anyway. Dad didn't want a party. He'd rather be in the arms of his Gilbertese girlfriend or getting pissed somewhere miles away from Lorelei.

'Your cousins are here now. They're asking where you are.'

'I just wanted to see the beach, I like it here.'

Lorelei paused in the shadows. 'Some of our relatives lived here once, long ago.'

The idea took a while to sink in. Lily turned to look up at her mother. 'You never told me that—do you mean they were lepers?' Lily said.

'Yeah, an old great granny, she was a leper, and her husband. No one alive knows anything about her anymore. She stayed here at the leper hospital with a granddaughter, one of my aunts. They all died during the war. Someone once told me that my auntie drowned. I'm not sure if it's true or not.'

'What were their names?'

'She was Edouwe. I've forgotten the old woman's name.'

'How come you've never told me before?'

'Didn't think you were interested.'

There was a heavy silence while Lily gauged her mother's mood. 'Ma, sometimes I think I hear voices in my dreams, of wailing women. You don't think it's her do you? Edouwe, I mean.'

'Shit, girl, where do you get these stupid ideas? You've been spending too much time with that thief Hector and his crazy *ibu*. You stay away from them, girl. That old man Riki is strange. He doesn't talk to anyone, turns and walks away when people go near. He's rude, he's no good. You keep away.'

'But Hector says…'

'No! Hector, too, my girl. He's a thief. You keep away. Stay at home where you're safe.'

Lily rolled her eyes. Yeah, at home with you knocking me round all the time? Stupid, fat witch, always telling me what to do. Stuff her—Hector was harmless.

'Come on, Lil, I want you to get the rice out and cook the breadfruit.'

Lily wanted to say, 'Why don't you do it yourself, you lazy bitch', but she saw the can of beer in Lorelei's hand and she didn't want to tempt fate. She stood up, brushed sand from her shorts and led the way back up the path to the clearing.

Joachim and Rongo were at the barbecue, turning sausages and chicken wings and waving the smoke away from their eyes.

Lily walked to the back of the Landrover and pulled out a big basin of breadfruit. She covered each fruit in foil then carried the basin over to the barbecue ready for

Rongo to cook the breadfruit in the ashes.

The next chore was the rice. It was one of the first things packed in the Landrover and she had to stretch out along the length of the vehicle to pull it towards her. She sensed a person behind her. She froze.

'Want some help?'

It was Eldon.

Her body was strung like a fishing line about to break. She leapt back to stand up straight and felt his body behind her, pushing up against her buttocks. He wrapped one of his chunky arms around her waist and pressed her against his groin.

'*Ngaitirre!*' she snapped, elbowing him in the chest and breaking free of his hold. As she spun around she yanked at the Landrover door to slam it against him, but he saw it coming and braced himself.

'What's the matter? I just asked if you wanted some help,' he whined, his brow wrinkling in earnest. He held his hands awkwardly across his fat belly as if he didn't know what to do with them, his stubby fingers patting and tapping nervously. Looks just like a dog that's been kicked, she thought.

'Get the rice out,' she snarled, backing away towards the barbecue. She could feel herself shaking and her breath was coming too fast. She knew she'd have to calm down, but she was furious. Safe, hey Lorelei? She snorted out her rage as she neared the barbecue. Stuff them! Stuff them both. One day, she swore to herself, one day she'd kill the bastard.

seven

Yamek District
30 December 1942

Tepu left the camp straight after he'd eaten, when night was already creeping into the sky. He made his way through the forest alongside Baringa Bay. To his left was the Ring Road and the beach. He dared not walk on the track for fear of patrols. Out on the beach he'd also be easily spotted from the pillboxes that lined the coast every mile or so.

Inside his trouser pocket the stone felt warm against his thigh. He trusted it to guide his feet, make his footsteps unheard, make his progress swift. Whenever he carried the stone his senses strengthened. He could hear not only the surf crashing on the reef but also the whisper of the retreating waves speeding back to the sea. Underfoot in the forest he felt the squelch of humus between his toes and knew by its consistency which part of the forest he was in. He saw clearly the forms and shapes of trees, fallen logs and rocky outcrops. All would have been merely vague shadows to him before. He was thankful for the stone's powers.

Tonight was a self-imposed test. Could he make it to the leper colony and back without being caught? It was a half hour walk along the track during daylight. He hoped to make it there and back again through the forest in less than two hours.

As he crept through the jungle he was alert to any sign of a Japanese patrol. High above him in the walls of the escarpment to his right was the Baringa Bay lookout, a bunker that many of the officers used. The track that led to the bunker was somewhere nearby in the forest. Voices rang out from the cliff top, muffled by the thick vegetation. Tepu was sure it was Japanese officers relaxing after a day's supervision in the sun.

He edged his way forward silently as he neared the section of jungle where the path to the bunker began. The forest was thinner here but there were lots of coral pinnacles to hide behind. Tepu knew, however, that they were hiding places for the enemy too.

A noise ahead made Tepu freeze. Someone cleared his throat and spat.

Should he go on? He couldn't just slink away without trying to reach the leper colony. Tepu took a deep breath and rested his hand against the stone in his pocket. It was still warm. The heat calmed him, helped him to think clearly.

He peered into the darkness. The silhouette of a sentry leant against a pinnacle, but Tepu knew there would be others stationed nearby. They never stood alone.

Tepu crouched behind a large rock and fumbled in the dirt until he found a few chunks of coral. He took aim and threw a pebble at the sentry's pinnacle.

Crack! It clipped the top of the pinnacle and ricocheted off at right angles.

The sentry jolted into action. He spun about and flourished his rifle. Another marine called from behind him. The sentry shouted in reply and pointed his rifle into the darkness well wide of where Tepu hid.

Summoning all his courage, Tepu hurled a second stone. It fell short of the pinnacle, thudding in the dust at the sentry's feet.

Tepu swallowed hard. He wished his second shot had been as accurate as his first.

More shouting followed. This time the other sentry emerged from hiding and prowled behind the first. They bent low over their weapons, scanning the gloom of the forest, alert to the slightest noise. To Tepu's horror they were coming towards him.

Anbwido
Monday 28 June 2004

Hector watched his grandfather sleeping at the edge of the porch, his back against a corner post, his head lolling on one shoulder. The island shirt he wore, once a vibrant blue and red, was now a faded rag with several buttons missing. His brown belly protruded where the shirt failed to cover him. As he dozed his thick purple lips trembled and his nose quivered. Hector thought his grandfather had the biggest lips and longest nose of anyone he'd ever seen, except of course for the Australian teachers and Christina and her dad. Their noses were thin and sharp like beaks.

Hector sat on the steps whittling a length of wood. This piece was one of his newest projects and he imagined it when finished as a long thin staff, probably not strong enough to support someone, but beautiful because of its curves and fineness. He liked the wild, twisted shapes that fallen branches made. Strewn on the beach, they were dry and bleached from the harsh sunlight. Did they all come from the few tortured looking trees that hung over the beaches on the island? Or maybe they were driftwood, resting after a journey of thousands of kilometres from the islands of Guam or the Gilberts.

He'd also found lightly weathered branches in his wanderings through the scrub near the house. The wood was always wet in the forest. It didn't take long for the jungle to turn everything into black soil.

He looked up from his work. The three girls were walking up the track from Decima's house towards the 'hut', as he and Riki called their home.

As they came nearer there was no mistaking them: Lily with her thick legs, Decima with her squeaky voice, and the long pale limbs of the Australian girl. They laughed as they walked along.

'Where you going?' Hector called out.

'Coming to see the chicken thief,' Decima said.

Riki stirred and opened his mouth, startled.

'It's OK, Ibu, we've got visitors.'

The old man straightened his shirt and eased himself

up into a standing position. He smiled at the girls, indicating the table at the other end of the porch.

'Come…sit,' he said.

Hector disappeared indoors to find water and food to share. In the kitchen he opened the old bar fridge: three bottles of water and a plate of tinned mackerel in tomato sauce stared back at him. He suddenly felt very aware of his poverty. If only they had more, to impress the girls and make him feel good. He got out the plate and rested it on the bench while he inspected the contents of the morning's rice pot. He heaped a few spoonfuls of rice onto the plate beside the fish and took it out to his guests.

The three girls were squashed together on one side of the table. Decima and Christina were smiling but Lily looked frightened. He saw her gaze go from Riki to the ceiling. He looked up to see what she could find fault with. Was it the floats and fishing nets hanging from the rafters? No, he knew his grandfather was the problem.

'Drink too, Hector,' Riki said.

Hector went inside again and fetched a chilled bottle of water and some cups.

'Are you looking for chickens?' he heard Riki ask the girls.

'Eh no, we're just going for a walk,' Decima said, winking at Hector as he came out with the water.

Shit, wrong one, he thought. Why isn't *Lily* winking at me? He settled himself beside his *ibu* and poured the water.

'You know Lily, Ibu? She lives down on the beach,'

Hector said. 'And this is Christina. She's here on holidays from Australia.'

The old man nodded at Christina then turned to Lily and smiled. 'I know Decima is my neighbour…you are Decima's friend, yes?

Decima interrupted, 'She's my cousin, Riki. Her mum, Lorelei, is my auntie.'

'Ah…and your father?' Riki said.

'Amos Fasiti, from here in Anbwido,' Lily said.

The old man nodded again, 'I know your father, a footballer in his youth…you have his face…same eyes I think.' He stretched out over the table and grasped Lily's stained hand.

Hector held his breath wondering what the old man was doing. Don't screw this up for me, Ibu, he thought. Lily looked startled, but she let the old man take her hand. The splash of purple skin contrasted with the leathery brown of the old man's.

'What happened to your hand?' Riki asked.

'Nothing,' said Lily, 'it's been like that since I was a baby.'

Riki kept nodding. 'This is an unusual mark. You are a special person,' he said, turning her arm gently to see the extent of the birthmark.

Lily wrenched her hand away and the old man let it go without resisting. He smiled at her, but said nothing. She stared at the floor. A long silence followed. He had to think of something to say or they'd leave.

'Have some water,' he said, conscious of his forced voice.

'We thought we'd go over to Anbwido for a swim,' Decima said, collecting the cups. 'But we said we'd show Christina some things from the war too.'

The old man looked at Decima coldly. 'Why do you want to do that?'

Hector came to her rescue. 'You know Ibu, tourism, and her dad's told her stuff about the war.'

Riki sighed, sat back in his chair and stared into a space beyond them all. His big purple lips moved back and forth, as flexible as bubblegum.

He always did this, Hector mused. The mouth movements were his pre-speech warm-ups. Here comes the speech of the day—how embarrassing.

Riki took a deep breath. 'The war, yes, there were marines here. I was just a young boy then. Just like Hector. Made us work. Made us do all their work. They were mean. We had nothing to eat.' He paused and turned to Hector, 'Do the girls want to see the hat?' he said. 'Go get the hat.'

Hector went into the kitchen. Above the fridge was a shelf that held rusty metal boxes, old cartridges and a battered tin helmet. He took the helmet and went back outside.

'See this, it's a Jap helmet,' he said handing it to Christina.

She turned the blackened metal over in her hands and felt the dints in it. 'Good protection. It looks like someone tried to shoot the soldier in the head.'

'Mum,' Riki murmured.

Christina passed the helmet over to Decima and Lily

who inspected it in silence.

'How did you survive?' Christina asked.

'We ate rats, lizards...we stole...stole anything we could. We did it to stay alive.' He took a sip of water. 'Not like now...kids thieving all day and night...think they can do whatever they like. Won't listen to the old people. Won't do what they're told. Are kids like that in Australia?'

'Some of them,' Christina answered.

'Tell us more about the Japs,' Hector said, steering the topic back.

'Swearing too. We never swore like that. We never swore like young people now.' Riki scratched at his stomach where it was exposed, coughed loudly, leaned to the side of the porch and spat over the side.

Hector saw Christina frown. He made a mental note: Australians mustn't like coughing and spitting. 'Come on, Ibu, tell us about the Japs,' he repeated.

'They were bad, brutal, evil men. They shouted at you...never let us be. If they caught you with any food, you must give it to them, then they flogged you...beat you with a lump of wood. But they stole...stole the island... stole our life. So many islanders died.'

The old man paused and swallowed back the pain of memories. He shifted in his seat and sighed.

'Did they have swords?' Decima asked.

Lily glared at her.

Again the old man paused, looked up and gulped the air. 'Yes, they had swords. They chopped your neck if they wanted to.' He was crying, Hector knew. Not openly like a child, but his eyes were wet and he blinked in an effort to stop the flow.

How would the girls react to this? The old man droning on and blubbering about his memories. No wonder Lily's family thought Riki was weird. But the three girls seemed transfixed by Riki's story. Lily had relaxed and was even smiling now. Maybe it was all right to mention the sword after all.

'I told you about the sword we found, Ibu. Do you think it was Japanese?' Hector said.

As soon as he said it he felt the sting of Lily's kick beneath the table. Above the table she scowled at him.

Riki grunted and wiped his eyes with the back of his hands. 'Could be,' he muttered. He gazed steadily at Lily and his voice shook as he spoke. 'I'd like to see it one day, my girl, just to look—no *pabwa*.' He pushed back his chair and moved to get up.

Lily's expression was troubled.

'You seen a Jap *yani*, Riki?' Decima asked.

Riki clutched at the balcony wall and almost stumbled.

'You OK, Ibu?' Hector asked, moving towards him. But the old man waved him away, sat back in his chair and took a deep breath.

'Ghost? Plenty ghosts on Tevua.' He helped himself to the food. 'I came back from overseas, from Majuro, I saw an old lady one day, a friend when I was young. She sat on the cemetery wall. I talked to her. She just smiled but she didn't talk. I walked away. Then I found out she died when I was overseas.' He smiled and his belly shook, like he was trying to stop himself from laughing. 'She's a ghost.'

'Are you sure it was a ghost?' Christina asked, frowning.

'Yes. I talked to the ghost, but I didn't know it!'

'Did she try to hurt you?' Lily asked.

'No, she was a friendly ghost, not like that witch in Baringa, she's evil.'

The group fell silent again. Hector picked at the mackerel with his fingers, pulling the tender flesh free and coating it in the sauce before eating it.

'How do you know if a ghost's evil or not?' Decima asked.

'You must ask yourself, was it evil when it was alive? My friend was not evil.'

'But how do you know, if you didn't know them when they were alive?' Hector said.

'Yeah,' said Lily, wiping rice from her lips, 'that witch is an old ghost. She might have been good when she was alive, but because her children were taken, she's angry. That's why she wants to steal other children.'

Riki stared at Lily before he answered. 'Some people die in so much pain, fear or shame, that even though they're dead, they walk the land they die on. They want peace, to set them free,' the old man said.

'Are there any Japanese ghosts on Tevua, Ibu?'

Riki snorted. 'I don't know.' His tone was gruff and he moved to get up once more.

No one spoke as he rose and the girls exchanged nervous glances. Hector had to keep him interested. 'Lily saw a ghost, just last week.'

This time Lily swore at Hector and Christina's mouth fell open. Hector wondered whether Lily would ever forgive him, now her secret was out. But Ibu was talking and it was so rare that he had to make the most of it.

'Where did you see it?' Riki's voice was a whisper.

Lily shifted in her seat but she didn't take her eyes off Hector. 'Near my house, just down there,' she waved.

'There is a pillbox nearby, yes?'

'Yeah, it's just down the beach from our house.'

'Then that must be the home of your ghost, he probably died in a bombing raid. Have you been there to feel the air?'

'What do you mean, "feel the air"?' Hector asked.

'She will know when she tries it. A cool breeze cuts your heart. You will feel its pain.' He smiled at her and patted his belly.

Hector was relieved: Lily seemed more relaxed now, engaged by Riki.

'He seems dangerous...angry or something,' Lily said.

'If he was a Jap he was cruel when he was alive.' The old man paused and thought for a moment. 'When you see him, what does he do?'

'He shouts at me, but I can't hear him.'

Riki smiled and nodded, 'He is silent. It is good.' Then he stopped and waved a finger at Lily's face. 'Don't tell anyone else about this ghost, my girl. They might think you are crazy, like me.' He turned and winked at Christina. 'This one, she thinks we're crazy.'

Christina shrugged and avoided Riki's eyes.

Lily and Decima laughed. The girls weren't so frightened of him now. Hector smiled too.

'I have one more question,' Lily said. 'Do you know anything about the lepers that were on the island?'

Riki's face twitched and he straightened himself slowly. 'They died,' he muttered and their conversation was cut short by the slow put-put of a motor scooter winding up the narrow track.

They all turned and looked down the path to see Lorelei, her fat frame bouncing on the small vehicle as it manoeuvred over the bumps.

'You come home, girl!' she shouted over the noise of the motor. 'You come home right now.'

Lily pushed away from the table. 'I've got to go, sorry.'

'Maybe tomorrow I'll come around,' Decima whispered to Lily as she left.

Hector watched Lily walk down the steps and get on the back of the scooter. Although it was difficult with Lorelei's bulk, she avoided touching her mother. Instead she kept her balance by holding on to the back of the seat. She looked like a dog when you shout at it: sullen and defeated. It wasn't the same Lily Hector knew at school, the fearless Lily. But Hector knew better than most people that sullen dogs bite.

eight

The marines came closer. Tepu held his breath. His pulse thundered through his body, urging him to run, but he dared not. They were only a few steps from where he hid. The slightest movement would mean capture or death.

Suddenly a flurry of wings swooped upon the sentries. A dozen black noddies whistled, dived and darted around the clearing as if disoriented.

The marines shouted, swinging their guns in the air. Shots rang out. In the confusion Tepu sprinted from his cover across the clearing and vanished into the night. He ran on as soundlessly as he could, terrified his breathing and the rhythm of his gait would attract attention. He only slowed down when he reached the hills at Anbwido.

It was a few minutes from there to the leper camp. He knew he should stop to give thanks to the great ancestor bird but he feared the witch ghost that roamed the hills and devoured children. He was no longer a child though;

surely she wouldn't harm him. He knelt under a huge tomano tree. Its night-time flowers filled his lungs with their sweet heavy scent. He closed his eyes, raised his hands and began the soft chant he had now perfected, 'Ancestor bird, I call you. Ancestor bird, I follow you.'

Within minutes the floating sensation entered his body. He opened his eyes and saw the phantom bird sitting on a branch above him. He wanted to say how grateful he was for his narrow escape but the power of the bird's green stare made Tepu's voice catch in his throat. He hoped none of the black noddies had been killed in the shooting.

'They sacrificed themselves to help me. How can I thank you?' he whispered.

The black tern ruffled its feathers and whistled in response. Then it turned its head in the direction of the leper colony, made a chattering sound and flew away.

Tepu heard a booming noise from down on the beach. He saw an orange glow in the direction the bird had just flown. Anbwido Leper Colony was ablaze.

Baringa Bay
Monday 28 June 2004

'This is Baringa Channel,' Decima announced, pointing down the hill. 'The channels are the only way to get boats in and out. They blasted them through the reef years ago. They're the safest places to swim because there are no rocks, but you have to watch the undertow.'

As they neared the beach Christina saw a broad

section of crystal blue water cutting through the reef. About a third of the way along, as it deepened, the water darkened. She gazed out to sea. Towering white clouds, which must have been tens of kilometres thick, plunged like giant cliffs into the horizon.

Christina couldn't wait to plunge into that crystal blue herself. The sun was fierce. They'd come from Hector's hut along the Witch Track and even though it was only a ten minute walk, sweat drenched her T-shirt and trickled down the back of her neck.

At the top of the channel was a concrete ramp. Christina spread out her towel. 'You can share mine if you like,' she offered.

'Don't need one,' Decima said. 'In a few minutes I'll be dry again.'

The two girls walked down the ramp to meet the water. Christina was surprised how warm it was, like a heated pool. She waded in up to her waist before duck-diving under. Instantly she felt cooler and wondered if it would drain some of the colour from her face. Hector had commented how red her face got just by walking. It didn't normally do that. Perhaps it was the humidity. Secretly she envied her new friends' colour. It would be nice to be so brown and not change from white to red so dramatically. She resembled a red-heeler, all freckles and strawberry-blonde hair.

'Lily and I were down here yesterday for her father's barbecue,' Decima said, 'except a bit further along.' She pointed to the right where dozens of coral pinnacles stood in the sand and the jungle spilt onto the shore. 'The leper colony used to be in there.'

Christina was horrified. 'And you go there for barbecues?'

'Yeah.'

'Aren't you scared?'

Decima looked puzzled. 'What of?'

'Catching leprosy.'

'Don't be silly! No one on the island has had leprosy since…since I don't know when. You can't catch it from the grass or anything.' She lay back in the water and let herself float in the swell.

Christina was silent. Wasn't leprosy that disease where body parts rotted away and fell off, bits like noses and fingers and toes? She'd have to quiz her father about it when she got home. 'I don't know anything about leprosy, except I think they can cure it now,' she said.

'See, no problem then,' Decima said smiling. 'Not like what my mum's got. She's really sick.'

'What's wrong with her?'

'She's got diabetes. She gets her blood cleaned out every few days…her kidneys don't work.'

Christina didn't know what to say. 'Will she get better?'

Decima shrugged.

There was another silence as they both drifted in the gentle waves. Finally Decima said: 'Do you have a boyfriend?'

Christina considered lying to impress her but decided not to. Decima didn't need to be impressed. She was straightforward and friendly, not like Lily. Perhaps it was because Decima had been to Australia before. She'd told Christina about her stay in Melbourne as they walked to the channel. Christina felt at ease in her presence.

'No...do you?'

'No.'

'What about Lily?' Christina asked. 'Is Hector her boyfriend?'

Decima shrieked. 'Eh, no! What a joke, Hector and Lily! Hector is only a baby.'

'They seem to spend a lot of time together.'

'They don't usually. It's just been this last week. Lily likes this boy at school, Jonah. He's from the other side of the island and he's really good at football.' Decima shook her head and laughed once more. '*Suh*! Hector and Lily, if Lily heard that she'd kill you.'

'I think she wants to anyway. I don't think she likes me,' Christina said quietly.

Decima laughed. 'She's like that with everyone, don't worry. It's just her way. Things are hard at home. Her mum's pretty mean.'

Christina remembered how Lily's mum had ridden up to Hector's hut and taken her away. A fat lady with a pissed off expression. Then she remembered Lily's bloodshot eye. She was too afraid to ask her about it, but it was obvious someone had hit her. Her cheek looked dark and swollen too. But what could she say? Hey, who's been bashing you? Lily's home life wasn't any of her business. But she'd try harder with Lily.

'I know where we should take you next!' Decima exclaimed. 'Come to the nightclub with us.'

'But I'm not eighteen.'

'Neither are we, but heaps of kids go. Not to dance; we go to watch.'

'Are you sure it's all right?'

'Yeah, the boys do it all the time. We just have to be more careful.'

'Careful of what?'

Decima grinned at her and winked. 'Careful our parents don't find out we're there.'

Christina wrestled with her indecision. Her dad wouldn't want her to go, that's for sure, but she didn't want to seem gutless in front of Decima. And anyway, they were only going to watch. What harm could it do?

'OK,' she said, grinning to hide her anxiety.

nine

Anbwido Leper Colony
30 December 1942

Tepu raced down the hill towards the fire. He could hear people shouting above the roar of the blaze. Flames grew tall and sparks of burning thatch twirled against the starry sky.

As he entered the colony he saw the clinic building and a small storage hut were alight. People stood and watched, their faces illuminated by the orange glow. The fire was already too big for them to extinguish. A few bags of flour and rice were all the lepers had managed to salvage. Tepu was relieved to see the sleeping huts untouched by the flames. He found Edouwe and her grandparents huddled together at the edge of the crowd.

'Are you all right?' he gasped.

The three of them turned to Tepu in surprise.

'Tepu, the curfew...' Edouwe began.

'You shouldn't be out after dark, it's too dangerous,' her grandfather said.

'I had to see if I could get past them,' Tepu whispered.

The old man nodded and patted him on the shoulder. 'Be careful then.'

'What happened here?' Tepu asked, pointing back to the blaze.

'The Japanese did this,' Mele said.

'We were all asleep but a patrol went by. They shouted and shot something, maybe a grenade or a shell. We don't know. It woke everyone up. Now the clinic is gone and our food supply as well,' Edouwe said. Tepu could tell she was struggling not to cry.

'They mean to make us starve,' Mele said. 'I thought they would leave us alone, but I fear they want us dead.'

'You won't starve, Mele. You can still fish the reef here. They're too scared to come into the camp or take any food you've caught,' Tepu said.

He hoped his words would reassure them, but he knew from his own meagre rations that food was becoming scarce. The old woman was probably right. Soon they would be fighting not just the Japanese but amongst themselves for a stunted coconut shoot or a small reef fish. Soon enough, people would begin to die.

Anbwido
Monday 28 June 2004

Lorelei slammed the door shut and pushed Lily forward into the lounge room. 'You stay inside—for the rest of the day! You hear me?'

Lily made for the nearest armchair and flung herself

down. 'You can't make me,' she snarled, sinking into the cushions.

Stupid little bitch, Lorelei thought, she's asking for a fight. Thinks she can do whatever she likes. 'You watch your mouth girl, or I'll smash it again,' she growled. She grabbed her daughter by the jaw and squeezed it hard, distorting Lily's face. 'You do what you're told, and I told you already, keep away from that crazy old Riki.'

'There's nothing wrong with him,' she mumbled.

Lorelei pushed Lily's head to one side and held it there. The girl breathed deeply and looked away from her mother's face.

Eyes like a frightened dog, Lorelei thought, squeezing harder, willing her daughter to flinch. She was not rewarded. As the tension grew Lorelei became conscious of the clack clack clack of the fan above them. 'Shut that noise up!' she shouted, pushing Lily aside and advancing on the fan controls. She fiddled with the knob until satisfied with the hum, then turned back to Lily. 'There's plenty wrong with that man, girl, believe me. He's not normal.'

'Like what?' Lily said in a surly voice.

Lorelei paused for a moment. How could she convince her? How could she make her understand that some men weren't safe? She wiped at her brow with the side of her hand and wished she had a beer in her to cool down. 'He's rude, Lily. He doesn't talk. People say he went for twenty years without speaking to anyone, not even his wife or children.'

'Well he spoke to me,' Lily said.

'And who are you, girl? You're not special,' Lorelei said, curling her lip and wiping her sweaty hands down the front of her dress. 'And what are you doing talking to white people? I don't want you getting any stupid ideas in your head.'

Lorelei knew all about what white people did, she'd seen enough movies. Plus she'd had her own encounters with them. They were all immoral and out of control. And they were always in those porno DVDs. No shame—white people had no shame.

She waddled over to the kitchen and took the broom from the corner. 'Plenty of housework to do, girl. Don't just sit there.'

Lily dragged herself out of the chair and snatched the broom from her mother.

Lorelei was relieved she'd won, but she wondered for how long.

ten

Yamek District
5 February 1943

Just before dawn Tepu woke to a strange sound like the buzz of a giant insect. Tarema heard it too. Together they emerged from the lean-to, stretched and looked up. The sky was a deep grey with a pink smear of light on the horizon.

The neighbours had also stirred from their sleep. Within moments everyone at Yamek camp was awake. They could all see the planes approaching, a swarm of black dots against the grey.

The droning grew louder; the hum filled the sky. Then came whistling noises, then the booming, so loud the ground shook.

Children scrambled for the protection of their mothers. Wailing babies added to the din and people's faces were tight with fear, alternately looking up then cringing with each blast. Tepu's mother knelt in the sand, holding her hands over her ears. He could see the terror in her eyes.

'They mean to kill us!' she cried.

'No, Mami, it's the Americans,' Tarema said, pulling at her shoulders, desperate to shift her.

'We must hide among the pinnacles,' one of the men shouted.

Tepu helped Tarema drag their mother to cover. Although the first few bombs landed close to Yamek, the main onslaught was further away. As far as Tepu could tell, the Americans were targeting the southwest of the island: the new runway they had spent months building for the Japanese. All their work would be blown away in one morning's raid. What a waste of their suffering, but what a sweet victory. Tepu didn't know whether to laugh or be sorry.

'The Americans have come to save us!' a neighbour shouted over the blasts.

Tepu's spirits lifted, but he could hear the big Japanese guns firing in retaliation and he doubted that freedom would come swiftly, nor without a price. He knew the Japanese would take revenge for the attack. With no Americans on Tevua, their wrath would fall on the islanders.

Anbwido
Tuesday 29 June 2004

The two girls sat in the *meneaba* beside Decima's house. A breeze cooled the sweat on their brows and necks.

'We're going to Melbourne next week,' Decima said.

Her deft fingers wound strands of Lily's hair into a thin braid.

'True? Poor Auntie Eide. I wish my mum was sick instead.'

'She's still your mum, Lil, even if she is nasty,' Decima mumbled.

'You don't get hit by her,' Lily said in a sullen tone.

'No...I'm sorry...anyway, she's getting so sick, she needs to go for tests.'

'So who's going?'

'Mum, Dad, me and the girls. The boys are staying here to look after the house.'

Lily stiffened. 'So where will I go?'

'Oh Lily, you'll be all right.'

All right, thought Lily. How? With Decima away, there was no one to stay with. For years now they'd slept over at each other's houses, usually one or two nights a week. Now she'd have to stay in her room alone every night. The lock didn't fasten properly. Eldon knew that. Besides, he could just as easily pull the louvres out. Two were broken already. Then there was the ghost. Lily felt panic begin to beat inside her.

· 'I wish you weren't going.'

'I know, but Mum needs me.' Decima carefully combed another section of Lily's fringe and began to plait again. In the silence Lily saw a pink frangipani fall to the crushed coral from the tree beside them. Like me, thought Lily, defenceless. She looked sideways at the tree through the beaded plaits already in place. That tree had always been there it seemed. She loved the fragrance that greeted her each time she stayed here, yet she hated its rounded limbs. Branches grey and swollen like dicks, stuck end to end like old toilet rolls.

'What's happening with Jonah?' Decima asked.

'Nothing.'

Lily thought about how he'd stared at her in class before the holidays. There was some kind of message in his eyes, she was sure, but she didn't think it was good enough gossip to tell Decima.

'I bet he'll be hanging round Black Hearts tonight. I told Christina we'd go.'

'We'll be seen,' said Lily. 'I'll be killed.'

'No one will see us if we walk along the beach.'

Lily thought for a moment. If she stayed the night at Decima's then her mum wouldn't know. 'Are you sure he'll be there?'

'My brothers reckon his family do the music there. He'd have to be there.'

'What about my face? My eye's still bloodshot.'

Decima scanned her face. 'It's almost back to normal and anyway he won't notice in the dark.'

'And what about your brothers, where will they be?' Lily asked.

'At a twenty-first party over the other side of the island.'

How perfect, Lily smiled to herself. 'Yeah, let's do it.'

That night Decima called outside Lily's lounge room window. 'Are you coming, Lil?'

Lily, her younger brother, Cyrus, and their father were

on the floor eating dinner. 'Yeah, wait,' Lily yelled back. She dusted sticky grains of rice from her fingers, crushed her soft drink can and bundled it up in the take-away paper in front of her.

'I'm staying at Decima's,' she said to her father.

Amos was motionless in front of the DVD player. He grunted but didn't look at her.

She got up from the floor and took her rubbish. Amos pushed his papers towards her in a feeble effort to help. He lay on his belly under the fan, his head pointed directly at the screen. Lily knew he wouldn't move for the rest of the night. Cyrus sat beside him, his mouth hanging open. He was only eight years old but he was already imitating everything their father and Rongo did. She'd seen him smoking a few times. She wouldn't be surprised to see him rolling around drunk any day from now.

She threw the rubbish in a cardboard box and met Decima and Christina at the back door. Lily could tell Christina was as nervous as a cornered rat. She was chewing her fingernails again. Thankfully, she'd found a T-shirt that was big enough to cover her midriff. Decima had told her to wear dark clothes so she would be hard to spot, but her white arms and legs were so obvious. Lily swore under her breath and hoped Christina wouldn't give them away. The only consolation was Christina's short hair. People would probably think she was a boy.

'Come on,' she said. 'Let's get out of here before Mum gets home.'

The girls scurried down the overgrown path towards the beach. Lily had it worked out well. All she had to do was get out of the house when her mum was away. Lorelei had left for bingo earlier in the evening—good riddance, piss off and don't come back. She would never have let Lily wander about at night, but Amos thought she'd be sitting around at Decima's. He was easy to fool.

Out on the beach the girls headed east in silence. They passed the pillbox they'd visited on the weekend. Lily shivered when she saw the pale dome in the moonlight.

'I hate this pillbox. It feels as though someone's looking at me through it,' she whispered.

'But no one's in it,' Christina said.

'I think Hector's grandfather's right though, don't you? I can feel someone in it, the air is different,' Lily said.

'Creepy,' Decima whispered.

The girls headed towards the waves, giving the pillbox a wide berth.

'You know how you think your ghost's a Jap,' Decima said. 'Well, how do you know he is? He might be just a Chinaman who worked in one of the restaurants or something.'

'He wears a uniform.'

'What sort of uniform?' Christina asked.

'He's got a coat…long sleeves and buttons…and badges. And he's got a belt…a plain brown belt. It's like he's all faded yellow…and he wears a little hat with an anchor on the front. I don't know, maybe you're right, but he seems like a soldier to me.'

He was small too, Lily remembered: bony and half-starved looking. She didn't like his face either. It was sallow and squashed, and his lips stuck out as if they were glued on as an afterthought. The bottom one seemed to hang. It was weird how those details were clear in her mind; but she didn't want to tell her friends everything. She knew Christina didn't believe her and it made her edgy. She took a deep breath and tried to put the ghost out of her mind.

'If we stayed here one night we might see him,' Decima said.

'Are you crazy?' Lily said. She stopped walking and glared at her cousin. She wanted to shake her and scream. Instead her voice came out all cold and low. 'I don't want to think about it, all right. It scared me. I don't want it to keep scaring me, do you understand? I don't want to keep talking about it.'

'OK, OK, I'm only trying to help,' Decima said. 'Come on, let's go,' she said to Christina and the two of them walked on ahead of Lily.

Lily rolled her eyes. She wished she'd never told any of them about the ghost. None of them could leave it alone. Why couldn't they just dismiss it as something she dreamt?

If only it was all a dream. She looked back at the pillbox and shuddered. Its entrance was an alien black mouth that gaped at her. A breeze crept in off the sea. Fifty metres away waves crashed against the reef in a rhythmic chorus that spilled warm water up onto the beach, washing over her feet.

Despite the warmth, Lily felt chilled. An eerie whisper called to her from the ocean. It was a girl's voice, thin and frightened. *Egirow, Egirow* it seemed to say. Or was it just the wind? She looked down in horror as a tingling sensation flowed up her stained arm. It was as if her birthmark was on fire. Terrified, Lily gave a stifled shout then ran after the others.

They'd already reached a rocky outcrop that jutted onto the reef. It was only another few hundred metres to the beach opposite the nightclub. A single streetlight lit the Ring Road and its glare filtered down on the girls.

'Are you OK, Lil? You look sick,' Decima said.

'I'm fine,' she lied.

They hid from view, ducking behind the rocks as cars drove past. The nightclub's music blared, competing with the sound of the waves.

'Listen, I think it's "Lucky Charmers." I love this song,' Christina said.

'They've always got good music here. They get the new stuff pirated before most people in Australia or New Zealand get to hear it,' Decima said.

'I'd rather hear it up close than lying on the rocks like a crab,' Lily said.

'You just can't wait to see if Jonah's there,' Decima teased.

Lily ignored her. 'Come on, we're nearly there.'

The three of them climbed over the rocks, then scampered along the sand to the path that led to the road.

They hunched down, waiting for the traffic to clear, then darted across to the carpark and hid beside the nearest Landrover. Security lights kept the area between the carpark and the nightclub bathed in a yellow glow.

Lily looked about for Jonah's brother's car. There it was, a battered, dark sedan with a white driver's side door, parked near the corner of the building. Her hopes rose. Maybe he was here, maybe she'd get lucky and talk to him.

'Let's move closer,' she said to the others, shouting over the music. Christina looked worried. Lily tried to reassure her, 'It's OK, kids always come and watch, see.' She pointed at the walls of the building. Every available window and doorway was crowded with boys jostling for a view.

'Hector's there,' Decima said, 'near the back door. Look, he's smoking with someone!' she laughed.

'Dumb shit!' Lily said, struggling to get a good view.

'It's Jonah, Lil,' Decima squealed.

Lily strained to see. 'I'll have to get closer,' she said. She ran up to the front row of vehicles and sat behind a motor scooter. Decima was right, it was him. And Hector. She could tell it was Jonah by the way he held his shoulders, and the muscled curve of his arms. How often she'd daydreamed about having those arms around her. She felt a rush of anticipation. She longed to go up and talk to him, but it was too risky. Someone would see and report her to Lorelei. She beckoned to Decima and Christina.

The two girls hesitated. 'Gutless cows,' she hissed. She'd have to attract his attention by herself. She picked up a handful of gravel and began throwing stones one by one.

eleven

Anbwido
19 February 1943

The American bombers had damaged the phosphate loading facilities, flattened administration buildings and destroyed many of the sheds that housed the Japanese food stores.

Bombs had also hit the runway, taking out three Japanese planes; otherwise the damage was minimal. The work gangs were deployed straight away to repair the surface.

The islanders' hopes that the Americans would liberate them dissolved. The bombers came without warning and vanished.

Tepu's fears of retribution were justified. The Japanese took revenge on the islanders for the Allies' attack. Weekly rations were cut to two small tins of rice and a piece of dried fish. Men were so hungry and weak that they stumbled as they worked. The marines pushed them to exhaustion and beat them when they fell. Tepu viewed the abuse as another test of his endurance. If he was truly a shaman, he would survive.

Once the runway had been restored the work gang moved to Anbwido. Now they bent their backs to dig trenches in the soil around the coast, while others built pillboxes.

It saddened him to be digging about like a crab in his old village. Apart from the Ring Road, Anbwido had become unrecognisable. None of the Tevuans' huts remained the same. Some had been transformed into makeshift barracks for the Japanese, but most had been ransacked, just like his own. The coconut palms and pandanus had long been stripped of their crops. Their leaves, tattered and dry, hung in the humid air like stiff flags.

Toiling in the sun on the afternoon of the nineteenth, Tepu witnessed two astonishing things. The first involved Edouwe and her grandmother.

The work gang was beside the beach, so close to the leper colony that Tepu could see the pinnacles of Leper Beach. At low tide two figures traipsed towards them, westward along the reef, pausing now and then at rock pools to collect unwary crabs or shellfish. They came closer. Tepu recognised Edouwe, although she had grown thinner and her ragged clothes flapped in the sea breeze. Mele, stooped and skeletal, followed her until they were within shouting distance of Tepu. The old woman began to sing.

'Our beautiful island, our home of joy...'

The workers looked towards the reef, but dared not

stop shovelling. The marines shouted at Mele and Edouwe to go away. Then one marine called out to the others, '*Rai-byo no onna.*' And immediately the rest backed away from the edge of the beach. Two marines picked up bits of coral and threw them at the women.

Undaunted, the old woman kept singing. 'We'll never leave our golden shores...'

One well aimed piece of coral smacked against Mele's side. Edouwe pulled her grandmother out of range of the missiles and added her own verse before Mele could interrupt. 'Don't fear for us, Tepuariki! We find enough, though we are hungry, we will see the devils gone!' Then they picked their way through the reef and out of sight.

The second surprising thing occurred after the women had left. Egirow began to behave strangely. He was agitated. Tepu noticed him wringing his hands. He feared Egirow was ready to launch into an attack, so he stayed alert as he worked.

When the supervising marines had their backs turned, Egirow disappeared. He walked uphill into the Anbwido forest in the direction of the Witch Track. He was gone for hours. Egirow normally only left the gang for short breaks unless a higher ranking officer called him away.

Where had he gone? There wasn't a bunker up there. Tepu knew the hills of Anbwido intimately. The Witch Track wound through the hills for miles with smaller paths leading off at intervals. Eventually the main track emerged onto the phosphate mining area on the island's plateau.

An idea crept into Tepu's mind. If Egirow went off alone into the forest, he was vulnerable. Anyone could hide behind a pinnacle and thrust a knife into his back. Repulsed by his thoughts of murder, he nevertheless resolved to monitor the marines' movements. With the help of the black stone he could ambush them one by one, if he had the courage. He thought once again about his grandfather's words. Was this his chance to prove himself, the ultimate test of strength and bravery?

Black Hearts Nightclub
Anbwido
Tuesday 29 June 2004

Lots of shell, there's always lots of shell at these dances, Hector thought. The girls lolled as they danced, round buttocks, bouncing breasts. He could imagine them full and soft, rolling around him as he danced. Dream on, he thought. Who was going to dance with him? The girls hated his busted face and he knew it.

He cursed at the memory of the dog attack that had left him sprawled in the dirt screaming, his face covered in blood. He'd only wanted to look at what the dog was eating. He was just a little boy then, not yet at infant school, but he could remember the snarl, the hot breath, the sudden lunge of sharp teeth. The vision still made him flinch.

Hector shut it out of his mind and stared through the barred windows into the darkened shed flashing with coloured lights. He saw the men swill warm beer and fumble with cigarettes. And they fumbled with the few girls they could reach. They staggered to find benches when they came back to sit down after a stint outside at the toilets. They were all big men so drunk they could hardly walk. How did they manage to dance? One guy hadn't even made it back to his seat. He lay on the concrete floor, arms spread out like Jesus on the cross. A huge landed tuna, still now, after vomiting underneath the bench beside him.

Boom, boom, boom—the bass thudded into the night. Hector pulled away to let another boy sneak a look inside. He glanced down the side of the shed at the groups of boys huddled around the barred windows. Some were so young they had to be held up to get a good view. This was Tevuan night life. This was where the gossip grew. If Hector watched carefully, he'd learn how to act cool, be a man and pick up girls.

He looked behind him. The light above the shed lit up the first section of the carpark. Rows of vehicles sat half in shadow. He saw a movement beside a Landrover at the edge of the carpark. Girls, trying to hide. He watched carefully to see if they moved again. There were three of them and Hector could guess who they were from their silhouettes and the pale limbs of one of them. Stupid! What was Lily doing out at night? Still, it was his big chance now to act cool in front of her. He'd go and find a cigarette, that's what he'd do.

Hector slunk along the wall of the shed. As he reached the corner of the building he looked towards the girls' hiding spot, but they'd faded into the shadows. He turned the corner, still looking over his shoulder when, bwack! He collided with another boy.

It was Jonah, the footy hero from Pago. He wore a sleeveless sports jacket with the hood pulled over his head and he held his cigarette between thumb and forefinger.

'Got a smoke, Jonah?' Hector asked, as cool as he could.

Jonah took a cigarette from inside his jacket and passed it and his own cigarette to Hector. Hector pressed the two together, pulling deeply and quickly, delighting in the red sparks that shone in the darkness. So cool, don't need a match—are you looking Lily?

'Want to come in?' Jonah asked. 'We'll stay over by the back door and you can choose some music.'

Hector hesitated. He wanted to see what the girls did next. Before he could answer, something flicked against his leg.

'Hey, who's chucking stones?' Jonah said.

Hector spun around. He could just make out a shadow behind one of the motor scooters. 'Over there,' he pointed, and together they walked over to the bike.

Lily got to her feet and stood awkwardly in the spotlight.

'Hi, Lily, what are you doing here?' Jonah said.

'Just checking the place out.' She fiddled with the scooter's mirror as she talked.

'I didn't think you'd come here,' Jonah said. He ran his fingers through his spiky hair and seemed to puff out his chest. A bit like a rooster, Hector thought. And then he understood. Lily was interested in Mr pretty-boy Jonah. And from the way he was talking to her, flashing his toothy smile and posing with his bulging biceps, Jonah was interested in Lily too.

Hector felt the hot sting of jealousy. He became oblivious to everything they said, and they said a lot. Lily smiled and fidgeted, all the while watching Jonah, and laughing at his jokes. She was too bold, so conspicuous in the light, her eyes shining in its glare. She was fearless, that's why she thrilled Hector so much. But now as he watched, he thought she was just plain dumb.

'I'd be careful, Lil. Cyrus said he'd come tonight,' Hector lied, interrupting them.

Lily looked at him with distaste, as if he was some kind of annoying insect. 'Bullshit,' she said flatly.

'No, true.' Hector had often seen her younger brother peering through the windows when the nightclub was rocking. He wouldn't be surprised if Cyrus did turn up at some stage tonight.

Lily turned to Jonah. 'I suppose I better go. Mum will kill me if she knows I've been here.'

Jonah nodded and smiled at her. 'Thursday then, at the Pago volleyball courts.'

'OK, see you there,' she said. Then she dashed back into the shadows.

Jonah slapped Hector on the shoulder. 'Well, you coming in or what?'

Hector made an excuse about a stomach-ache and strode off home. His head spun with rejection. Why Jonah? Why pretty-boy Jonah? Thursday, eh—Thursday they had a date. Well Hector knew what to do. He'd turn up too, and do his best to make sure that Jonah looked like a shithead.

twelve

Yamek District
6 March 1943

Tarema returned to the lean-to at sunset carrying a large orange shape, a ripe pumpkin. He set it down in front of their mother who stared at it vacantly. Tepu didn't like her reaction. Over the past few weeks she'd done a lot of sitting and staring. Now she'd been presented with the equivalent of a treasure chest: a whole pumpkin. His mouth watered just looking at it, but she didn't even blink.

'Where did you get it from?' Tepu asked his brother.

'They steal our house, I steal their pumpkin,' he said, leaning heavily on his knife, slicing the vegetable in two.

Tepu couldn't help but laugh, only the seriousness of the crime changed his tone. 'They'll catch you, Tarema, and then they'll hurt you.'

'They won't catch me, I move like a rat in the night.'

Tarema was thin and agile, and his nose was pointy. Tepu could imagine him twitching it like a rat. 'Yes, but rats gnaw and keep people awake. One day a quiet cat will be waiting. Be careful, Tarema.'

'I will. What about you? You walk around the forest at night, too. But I never see you come back with any spoils. What are you up to?'

Tepu considered telling him about the ancestor bird. Then he thought better of it. Tarema would only want to come along. He'd ruin things, frighten the bird away or maybe it wouldn't come at all. Then Tarema would think he was crazy.

'I'm scouting the forest, looking for patrols. One day I'll lay a trap for them,' he said.

Tarema's face lit up, excited at the thought of sabotage. 'I'll come with you.'

'No, it's best if I work alone. What if they catch us both, then what good would it do?'

Tarema looked offended. 'You don't want me to come because you're really a spy, right?' he whispered.

'Don't ever accuse me of such a thing,' Tepu spat.

'Well, prove to me you're not. Take me with you tonight.'

Anbwido
Wednesday 30 June 2004

There she goes, off to the shower block. She's trying to avoid me, Lorelei thought. She's stayed at Decima's no doubt, but who knows what sort of mischief they'd been up to. They probably met with her thief of a boyfriend late in the night.

Lorelei hated it when Lily didn't come home to sleep. It was OK when Lily was a child, but now she was a young woman, she couldn't be trusted. Neither could Decima. Besides, they had a room for her here and even if Amos wasn't home at night, then Rongo and Eldon took care of the place, made sure no boys came prowling about. She was really slipping, young Lily. She needed a reminder, she needed sorting out.

Lorelei pushed herself up from the armchair. Her insides were queasy from too much beer the night before. She'd have to go to the toilet anyway, she'd catch up with Lily when she came out from the shower block.

As Lorelei walked to the kitchen her head pounded with every step. She held her hands to her head and squeezed in a futile effort to stop the pain. Why did she do it? She had to tag along with Daphne, had to go and drown her disappointment from the bingo. Still, one day she'd win. One day she'd win the thousand dollar jackpot or a fridge.

Yeah, a new fridge, that would be excellent. She opened the old one and sniffed at the cool air. She looked for comfort, but there was nothing: no beer, nothing except cold rice. She slammed the door shut and examined its surface. There were rusty spots and patches where the white paint had chipped away. Dots of black mould grew down the sides. Yeah, she could do with a new fridge. And when she'd won it, she'd stock it full of beer and fish and throw a party.

Shit, what a party it was last night! All that dancing, and singing too. No wonder she felt sore all over. And what time was it when she got home? Maybe after four in the morning, but her sons were asleep in the lounge room in front of the DVD player as she lurched down the corridor to her room. And in her bedroom there was nothing but the mattress on the floor and a crumpled sheet. Amos was missing again. Why didn't the bastard stay home and look after the kids? But no, once again he'd gone to the shanty town in Dabweg where his young lover stayed. Lorelei wouldn't see him till late Wednesday night, if she was lucky. Amos the stupid arsehole, he was never home, never did his share.

She walked outside into the midday sun and screwed up her face to block out the glare. She headed towards the shower block. The door opened.

Lily stepped out, holding a towel. Her hair was tied to the side in a thick wet plait soaking her T-shirt.

'Where do you think you're going, princess?' Lorelei snarled, grabbing her daughter by the arm.

'Nowhere.' Lily tried to pull away from her and skidded in the coral. Her towel fell in the white sand that powdered her feet.

'Nowhere? Like off to see your little boyfriend.' Lorelei began pulling her towards the house.

'What do you mean?'

'Is that where you were last night, you *trut*—off with that chicken thief?'

'I was not, don't be stupid. I was at Decima's.' Lily tried to wriggle free but her mother's fingers pressed into her arm.

Fury boiled inside Lorelei. 'Stupid, am I? You dare call

me stupid. Don't you talk to me like that, you *trut*.' Lorelei dug her fingers in harder, determined to make her daughter cry out. She would suffer for the insult.

'Let go of me!' Lily screeched, pulling away.

Lorelei anchored herself in the gravel and tried to haul Lily back towards her, but she was surprised at her daughter's strength. 'Get in the house!' she screamed at her.

The woman's face was warped with rage. If only she could get a good grip on Lily, she'd thrash her till she bled. She'd hit her so damn hard she wouldn't be able to walk. But the stupid girl had sunk low into the coral threatening to topple Lorelei over.

She shouted down at her in a blast of alcoholic breath, 'Get up, you stupid bitch!'

Lily clawed at the loose coral with her free hand. As Lorelei tugged at her, Lily threw a fistful of crushed rock and dust into her mother's face.

'Eeeooow!'

Lorelei recoiled as the gravel flew at her, but she was too late. The grit bit into her eyes, stinging as she covered her face and howled, furious that she'd been outwitted.

thirteen

Yamek District
6 March 1943

Tepu stared at the ground for a long time, avoiding his brother's eyes. He knew the night-time absences must have looked suspicious. He didn't want to take his brother into the forest and scare off the ancestor bird, but he didn't want Tarema to think he was a spy. Tarema's words hurt him more than he was willing to show. There was no other way to prove his innocence except to take Tarema with him.

'OK, tonight, after she sleeps,' Tepu whispered, glancing towards their mother who sat at the edge of the lean-to, staring into the darkness.

Later, when they heard her soft snoring, the boys crept out into the forest. It was a cloudless night and they made good progress, thanks to Tepu's knowledge of the terrain.

Soon they came to a rough track Tepu had cut through the vegetation at waist height. Tepu had to crawl through most of it but Tarema, being smaller, simply crouched to keep up.

'You must never show anyone this track,' Tepu said, 'it's our secret.'

'Where does it lead to?'

Tepu didn't tell him about his small shrine in the pinnacles where he went to chant. Instead he told him about what lay beyond, high in the cliff.

'There's a Jap camp on top, where the officers rest. I've scouted around the bottom of the cliff and I know a few ways to climb up. It's steep and overgrown and they hardly ever patrol it from this side. I guess they think it's inaccessible.' He held his fingers to Tarema's mouth. 'Listen, you can hear them. I think they all get drunk up there.'

'Let's go up!' Tarema could scarcely contain his excitement.

'It's not safe, they might hear us.'

'Not if they're drinking they won't,' Tarema whispered, slipping away from Tepu's warning grasp.

'Tarema, come back!' Tepu called as loudly as he dared. He cursed after him. Why did he let his brother manipulate him? Now Tarema would be caught for sure, or fall and injure himself and it would be he, Tepu, who was to blame. He would have to stop him. Summoning his courage, he scrambled along the track after him.

Lily ran across the road and headed for the Witch Track. She knew her mother wouldn't follow her, but she wanted to be as far away as possible. Before she knew it she was on the path that led to Christina's house. Better there, than at home with Lorelei. Besides, her mum would never think of looking for her in Government Settlement. She smiled with relief at her escape from Lorelei and rubbed her arm. It was throbbing from the attack. The other thing to smile about was how her mother knew nothing about Jonah.

She couldn't believe how bold she'd been attracting his attention last night. But it had worked; he'd come over to talk to her. When she'd analysed it all with Decima, they both believed he'd talked to her as if he couldn't get enough of her eyes. 'He likes you,' Decima said, and Lily had asked her again and again to explain why she thought so. And every time Decima answered, Lily felt her chest bursting with pride. He'd talked to her about the music, tried to convince her to come inside, offered her a cigarette. But she'd been frightened and Hector had warned her about Cyrus and told her it wasn't safe.

Bullshit Hector. She shouldn't have believed him. She hadn't seen Cyrus this morning but she was certain he'd stayed home last night with Amos. Dumb shit Hector. Maybe something would have happened if she'd stayed there with Jonah. But really she knew he was right to warn her away. There were too many eyes in the dark.

And the funny thing was, Lorelei still thought Lily was

Hector's girlfriend. Ha! The idea suited her well, kept Lorelei misinformed. Her mother would never know that she and Jonah had arranged to meet at the volleyball tomorrow. She tried to hold that moment in her head for as long as she could. Me, me—he wants to see me! She was so happy she wanted to shout.

'Hello!' Christina said, startling Lily as she approached the Lowrys' back door. Christina walked out from the wash house, her pale thin arms straining to carry a load of wet washing.

'Hi. You got in all right then?' Lily said awkwardly. They'd walked her home along the Witch Track last night with the torch light failing. Bad batteries, Christina had said. It didn't matter that Decima swore she'd just bought them. No matter what they said, they couldn't convince Christina that the Witch Track was haunted.

'Yeah, Dad was waiting up for me but I told him I'd been at Decima's. I don't think he guessed anything.' She hauled a wet sheet onto the line and began pegging it out.

'Dad didn't get the washing finished this morning, so I have to do it.'

Lily was shocked—Christina's dad did the washing! Amos had never done any housework in his life. Well, men just didn't do any in Tevua. Washing was a woman's job.

'Want to go for a walk?' Lily asked.

'Where to?

Lily shrugged. 'We'll see if Decima's at home.'

'OK, just let me finish hanging this up.'

'Sorry if I'm disturbing. Can I help?' Lily said.

Christina grinned and handed her a peg. 'Sure. I don't like doing the washing and you're not disturbing me. Besides you're welcome here anytime.' Then she added with a serious tone, 'whenever you need to, you know… escape.'

Lily was astonished. What did Christina know? Had Decima talked about Lorelei? Maybe she guessed anyway because of Lily's black eye, or the red marks on her arm where her mum had grabbed her. Lily shrugged again and mumbled a thankyou.

Lorelei had always said white people looked down on Tevuans: exploited them, abused them. Although Christina hardly knew her, she was offering friendship and hospitality. Not at all like what her mother had warned.

Twenty minutes later they reached Decima's house, only to find it shut up, a contrast to the noise and chaos of that very morning when Lily had left. She called at the front door and listened for any movement. Nothing. Frustrated, Lily swore and slapped her hand against the doorframe. Where were they? Australia? No, the plane didn't leave until tomorrow. It must be Auntie Eide. Something must be wrong.

'They're at the hospital,' Hector called from the track. 'I saw them leave about half an hour ago. Eide blacked out. Come to my place. I've got cold water.'

Lily scowled. Hector was beginning to irritate her. She wanted to talk about last night again with Decima, not hang around with him.

'OK,' Christina said, 'I'm dying of thirst.'

Lily opened her mouth to object but Christina was already walking up the track to Hector's hut. Reluctantly, Lily followed.

Hector's grandfather was unpacking fishing gear from his jeep.

'Catch anything, Ibu?' Hector asked.

'A bad day, just one rainbow runner. I gave it away.' The old man turned to look at the girls and smiled his rubbery smile.

Lily returned the smile but she came no closer to the house. Her mother's words reverberated in her mind: Riki was crazy and she shouldn't associate with him. But why should she believe anything Lorelei said? All her mother wanted to do was keep her in the house and thump her.

If she could think of an excuse to leave then she and Christina could go somewhere else. But how would she convince Christina? Her new companion was happy to spend time with Hector and Riki. It would be rude to drag her away, just like her mum had done to her. She decided to wait for the right moment.

'Never mind, Ibu. We want water, it's so hot today,' Hector said as he disappeared inside.

The old man chuckled, 'Go ahead. It's a good day for swimming at the channel, Hector.'

'You take us!' Hector said from the kitchen.

'Well, wait for me to finish,' Riki said and he walked around to the back of the hut.

Hector motioned from the door for the girls to come

forward. Lily hesitated, but followed Christina to the steps of the hut and drank the cold water he offered. The chill was like a thread of ice snaking down her throat. If she was this hot now, imagine what it would be like at the channel? It would be cooler in the forest.

'How far away from the channel is that bunker you told me about, the one with the bath?' Lily said.

'Not far, the entrance is right near the restaurant on the bay,' he said.

'We could go up to that bunker instead of swimming,' Lily suggested. Exploring the forest was the best time she'd had with Hector.

'OK,' Hector nodded. He shouted around the side of the hut, 'Ibu, how about we go for a walk in the forest, to a bunker?'

Riki appeared at the opposite corner. He was draped in a huge fishing net and carried an old jerry can. 'Where?' he asked.

'Baringa, you know the one up on the cliff.'

Riki raised his eyebrows in agreement. He walked up the steps and put the fuel in the kitchen. Then he pulled the net from his shoulders, reached up to the rafters and threaded it through. 'I might be a bit slow, though,' he said.

Old bleached car bodies marked the beginning of the trail. Hector pushed past them and through the hanging vines and chest-high shrubs that blocked the track. Beyond were two pinnacles like guardians at the gate. He slipped behind one, hiding from his grandfather and the girls.

He ambushed them as they drew level.

'Whaha! I'm a ghost!'

Lily jumped back, her mouth wide with fright, and fell against Christina. They toppled to the ground in a tangled heap.

'Shit!' Lily gasped and the three of them erupted with laughter.

'You should have seen your face,' Hector said as he helped Lily to her feet.

She pushed him aside and swore at him.

Christina stood up, brushing soil from her clothes. 'We'll have to get him back later, Lil,' she smiled.

Riki coughed behind them. 'The path is overgrown,' he said in a strange hollow voice. He looked about slowly, his eyes troubled and weary. Then he began a rhythmic muttering that Lily couldn't understand.

She turned to Hector, but he shook his head, frowning at her and Christina to silence them.

Lily felt nervous. Her mum was right, there was something creepy about Riki.

The group trudged along a marshy floor that rose towards the darkness of the scrub. Mud oozed over the edges of their thongs and tiny black insects hovered in clouds about their ankles.

Fern outcrops hugged the bases of rocks and pinnacles that bordered the path through the black soil. The trees made a canopy that let in shafts of sunlight, each illuminating clumps of fern in a vivid glow. Everything between these pockets of green looked faded in the bronzed light. To their left the ground rose steeply and a hedge of tree hibiscus partially hid the ridge that loomed before them like the wall of a castle.

They plunged through the hibiscus. With each step Hector took, another branch flung back to whip Lily in the face.

'Watch it, arsehole. Do you want me to follow or not?' she said.

Hector chuckled. 'We're nearly through it. You should have brought the sword to cut a path. The bush grows back so quickly.'

'Perhaps we'll find another sword here anyway,' Christina said.

'What do you mean?' Lily asked.

'Well, if they had a bath up here, it was obviously a special place for the officers. And if they were the only ones who had swords...'

Lily still couldn't work Christina out. Was she just a smart arse? How much did she know, or thought she knew? Did Lily know less about her own history than this girl who had been here a week? People didn't talk about the history of Tevua. They were more interested in talking about football or fishing or music or sex, or just getting drunk and being stupid. History was dull in comparison.

The vegetation cleared and the ridge appeared before them: a steep, grey rise, dotted with huge coral boulders, each bigger than a large pig.

In the yellowed light the air was still and oppressive. Lily couldn't hear the familiar scratch of crabs or the scurry of lizards, just the drone of Riki's muttering as he lumbered behind them.

'Up there in the rocks,' Hector said, pointing, 'that's where the Jap soldiers hid.'

'Pretty good camouflage,' Christina said. 'You'd never guess there was anything there except a cliff.'

'We're going up there?' Lily asked, full of trepidation.

'It's easy,' Hector called, bounding up the slope.

Lily climbed steadily. It was so steep she had to pull herself from one pinnacle to the next tier. Her leg muscles burnt with exertion. Her lungs heaved. She wanted to stop, but she wouldn't dare let Hector show her up like this. He was only a few tiers above her, perched on a boulder like a bird. She inhaled sharply and willed herself onwards. Sweat trickled down her cleavage, pooling at the band of her bra, and a sweaty moustache had formed on her upper lip. She licked it away. Behind her she could hear Christina panting too.

'How much further?' Lily gasped as she reached Hector. She noticed the sheen of sweat on his temples. The humidity had slowed him too.

'Not far,' he said, watching his grandfather's progress. 'Come on, Ibu. You're nearly there,' he called down the hill.

The old man stepped his way up the slope, his breath coming in loud puffs. As he climbed, he used the pinnacles to haul himself up, as Lily had done. She watched the muscles of his long arms ripple in the muted light. Long ago, she thought, he would have been a tall thin youth.

When Riki reached them, Hector nodded towards a huge rock at the base of a coral ledge that jutted out about three metres above them. A young beach almond had established itself right on the edge, its roots encasing the cliff like a badly woven fishing net.

'We've got to get up there,' he said. 'Watch where I put my hands and feet—then follow that pattern. It's the easiest way.'

Riki was still puffing, but his mumbling had stopped. His lined face was covered with sweat. He used one finger like a windscreen wiper to clear the sweat away, then he shook his head and his shoulders slumped. 'I don't think I can,' he said. 'You three go ahead. My legs are tired. I cannot climb.'

'Are you sure?' Hector urged him. 'If you rest a while, you'll make it.'

'I will sit here and wait for you,' he said, smiling. 'You will tell me what you find.'

Lily imagined Hector's *ibu* in his youth, climbing coconut trees and cutting the young shoots to collect toddy. But now he was crumpled and worn and his belly heaved as he caught his breath. He didn't seem so weird now he was exhausted like her, but she was glad he was staying behind. It wasn't just Lorelei's warnings. There was something about his manner that spooked her.

The rock at the base of the cliff was waist high. Hector jumped up then looked down at the girls. 'Once we get over this cliff, it's much easier,' he said.

Lily hitched her skirt above her shorts and clambered onto the rock. She watched Hector scale the cliff face in front of her. He reached up to his right for a handhold and found a notch to the left for his foot. Two more similar manoeuvres had him within reach of the sapling.

He clasped a root and heaved himself up towards the trunk. Once he'd caught the base of the trunk he pulled himself up over the ledge. Then he stood beside the sapling and coached the girls as they made their way up to join him.

'Wow, what is this place?' said Christina, her eyes wide like a big bonito.

Their ledge formed a small platform out over the forest.

'My old school teacher says it's where the Japs were,' Hector said.

'The sentries stand there and look down to see if anyone is coming,' Riki called from beneath them.

Hector walked to the edge and crouched behind one of the large boulders that formed a natural barrier to hide behind. 'Tck, tck, tck!' he pointed his arm into the air and shot off an imaginary round of ammunition.

Lily laughed at him. 'You're like a little kid,' she said. Then she shivered as the air around her cooled. She looked up for the telltale change in the clouds, but the forest canopy blocked out the blue. She glanced at Christina whose nervous eyes were also scanning the treetops. Even Riki was gazing about uneasily. Hector was still shooting imaginary invaders with his invisible machine gun.

'Shut up, you idiot, and listen for a minute,' Lily shouted. 'Can't you feel it?'

Hector stared at her blankly. 'What do you mean?'

She shuddered as a tingling sensation crept down her body. 'I can feel *them*. The soldiers, guarding the way. Their ghosts.'

Hector looked towards his grandfather. 'Is that what you mean, Ibu? Can she feel the air?'

The old man raised his eyebrows and brought a finger to his lips.

'They are here, Hector,' he said, 'the air is thick with ghosts here.'

fourteen

Baringa District
6 March 1943

Tarema scaled the cliff face like a lizard on a rock. Tepu followed, terrified that at any moment one of them would lose their footing and tumble. He was glad it was too dark to see how far they'd climbed, but poor visibility meant they had to feel their way, sometimes doubling back when there were no handholds. The rocks were jagged and tore at their exposed skin. Tepu was thankful that his hands and feet were tough after labouring on the work gangs, but he worried how Tarema's hands were faring.

The noise grew louder as they neared the top. They could hear someone speaking rapid Japanese while another shouted. The brothers froze—had they been spotted? Tepu's heartbeat thundered at his throat. He held his breath.

A long silence followed, then the sound of many Japanese voices, someone coughing and a group of men chuckling.

Tepu exhaled. His legs shook.

'Come on, Tepu, we're nearly there,' Tarema whispered.

Tepu struggled after him, blinking away the falling debris dislodged by his brother's feet. Moments later Tarema stopped and Tepu hoisted himself up beside him. They had reached the top of the cliff. The Japanese voices were very close now, perhaps only a few feet from where they perched.

Tarema was about to peer over the edge when Tepu caught him by the shoulder.

'No, I must do it. I am older,' he whispered. Gingerly, he raised his head. Before him was a tent peg which held down one corner of a large tarpaulin. The tarpaulin formed a makeshift roof over a natural basin in the rock. About a dozen marines sat on the ground talking and drinking in the glow of a lamp. He recognised one face. It was Egirow. The Lieutenant drank from a large bottle, listening to his fellow officers and occasionally saying a few words.

'They drink while we starve,' Tarema whispered at Tepu's ear. Tepu was so engrossed he hadn't noticed his brother at his side.

'Get down,' he hissed, pushing Tarema back. Unbalanced, the boy slid, gasping and clutching madly for a handhold.

The noise made the marines turn. Someone shouted an order and they all rolled onto their stomachs, drawing their revolvers. A dozen pale faces squinted into the darkness, directly at Tepu.

Hector gulped at the humid air that hung around him. A sinister chill had come from nowhere, pawing at the sweat on his head and chest. He was unsure about going on, but Christina jolted him back to a kind of courage by her words: 'Must be a storm coming.'

Despite her scepticism about ghosts she looked frightened, as if she thought someone was watching her.

'So where's the bath?' Lily said hoarsely, pulling at Hector's shoulder.

'We go this way,' he said, pointing to a space behind the sapling. A path led to a cleft in the rock. Inside, limestone cliffs formed the walls of a narrow corridor. They walked single file down the curving path. The carpet of leaf litter, several centimetres thick, silenced their footfalls.

'Our teacher said this might have been an old reef, millions of years ago. Then volcanoes put a crack in it,' Hector said.

Lily snorted. 'You lie. There are no volcanoes here.'

'That's what he said. He told us all about this place. He said only one soldier at a time could come through this path. He said it was good for an ambush.' Hector looked up and imagined jeering Japanese high above, pointing their rifles at him. He would have been dead in an instant, like a squashed piglet on the road. Then all the blue flies would come and sit on his eyes and mouth. Dead Tevuan boy, move no more.

The path opened into a clearing as the two walls of

rock veered off in opposite directions. An old lime tree shaded the clearing and plenty of sour-sob seedlings struggled for a patch of sunlight. Beyond them the scrub was thick again.

Hector pushed his way through the bush, skirting the line of the right ridge. The girls followed as he plunged into the greenery again.

The ridge formed a wall, higher than any building Lily had ever seen. Its steel-grey surface was pock-marked with holes and crannies. The wall continued around in a curve. They kept close to the ridge for several paces, then Hector stopped and pointed to a recess in the wall. 'Look, can you believe it?'

Christina shook her head. A rusted white tub, filled with sixty years of mud and leaf litter, sat like a throne in the rock recess.

'How did *that* get *here*?' Lily's eyes were wide with astonishment.

'They must have dragged it up here. Well, forced slaves to drag it up here,' Christina said.

'Slaves?' Lily and Hector said in unison.

'Yeah…On of Dad's mates reckons the Japanese forced most of the locals to work as slaves.'

Hector could just imagine a soldier sitting in the bathtub, his pale body lifting a tin of water. He could see the water trickle down the sides of his head and his eyes would close for an instant. Then he would shake his black, stubbled head and his bottom lip would drip, drip, drip the last of the water—precious Tevuan water, while the islanders starved.

A rage of injustice seethed in him. He wanted to shout or swear into the forest, but stings like hot needles pierced his feet. He flinched and looked down. Dozens of orange-red ants crawled over his thongs. He brushed them away, stamped his feet and jerked sideways in a crazy dance.

'You look stupid, you idiot,' Lily laughed. She moved back from him, then stumbled to one side as she tripped over an old bottle. 'Shit!' she yelled.

'Who's stupid now?' Hector muttered. 'See, I told you they had beer bottles up here.' He pointed to where a few brown bottles lay beside the curved legs of the bathtub. Hector picked up the one Lily had tripped over and turned it in his hands. The neck was broken and inside he could see the same filth that filled the bathtub.

'Are you sure it's a beer bottle? Maybe they drank sake,' Christina said.

'What's sake?' Lily said.

'It's a Japanese drink, some kind of alcohol.'

'I don't know, can anyone read their writing?' Hector rubbed his fingers over the Japanese markings on the glass and handed it to Lily. 'Whatever it was, they got drunk.'

'Shit,' Lily said. 'They must have sat here and drank beer in the bathtub while the rest of them…' she screwed up her face and paused while the realisation hit her, 'they beat up our relatives. What arseholes!' she shouted, and she hurled the bottle at the bathtub. It smashed against the side with a clunk, spattering humus and glass everywhere. Her laughter was strident and she looked at her companions. There was cold fury in her eyes.

Christina didn't laugh. Nor did Hector. He felt afraid

in his gut and he wished she hadn't smashed the bottle. He was sure Ibu would have liked to keep it. The air around them cooled once more and Hector looked to the sky, noted the dimmed light and knew it was about to rain.

'Come on, we're nearly there,' he said.

He forced his way through another curtain of dense scrub and a small maze formed by a rocky outcrop. The girls followed a few paces behind. A distant boom sounded and the roar of a tropical downpour fell on the leafy roof above them.

Big droplets of rain spilled down from the waterlogged leaves onto their sweaty limbs. Drip, drip, drip—the rain soaked their shirts and Hector felt himself shiver.

'It's just up here,' he shouted over the noise of the rain. He smiled at how good Lily looked with water streaming down her face.

Up ahead there was a natural cave in the limestone ridge. Hector ran to the opening and crouched inside. Lily was beside him in an instant, squatting under the low entrance, edging closer to him. The cave was tiny, about the size of a small car.

'Move over, I'm soaking,' Christina said as she squashed in alongside them.

'Is this it?' Lily said peering around the cave in the gloom. The dusty floor was littered with old ammunition cartridges.

'No, the bunker is behind, through the crack in the ridge at the side there.' He pointed at the crevice they'd just passed.

Hector ran back out into the pass, then ducked under a low rock face that stuck out at knee height. As he entered the bunker he was aware of a cool chalky sensation that lingered at his lips. The air was dry and powdery. A pale light filtered into the chamber from a broad slit in the wall opposite. He moved towards the makeshift window and turned to watch Lily's expression as she entered. He saw her feet first, then her head ducked down and she crawled in after him.

'*Ai-ye-we!*' Her eyes were as wide as pipi shells. She pulled herself up and moved over beside him.

'You can't see much of the bay,' Hector said, indicating the overgrown trees that obscured the view, 'but here they watched for battleships.'

Christina came in next and she whistled at the view. 'You can see for miles up here!'

Hector gazed out, imagining US warships or even bombers approaching in the sky. These days there might only be a small boat, a dark smudge on a velvet sea, someone out catching fish for their families. Just like his *ibu* did every chance he could. But in this weather, the waters of the bay were black against a grey sky and no smart fisherman would get in a boat.

'What's out here?' Lily said. She crawled through a small opening which formed a ledge on the cliff side, perpendicular to the bunker. Hector joined her and together they sat in silence for a few minutes, watching the rain fall.

'It's great up here, Hector. It's worth the climb.'

'I know. It's my special place.'

135

Hector looked at her but he couldn't catch her eye. She was totally absorbed by the view. He thought she looked so beautiful sitting with her knees drawn up under her chin, her face wet with rain.

'How often have you been up here?' she said.

'I don't know. A few times. Ibu came up once. He found a metal lunchbox and a helmet, plus some broken bottles, but the climb's too much for him now.' He paused and looked at her again.

'Hey guys, you should see what's in here!' Christina called from above.

'She's found the tunnel,' Hector said, 'come on.'

He dropped back into the bunker and clambered through a narrow space that led back into the cliff. It was a passage that slanted upwards and was only a few metres long. Hector avoided the jagged flecks of rock that poked out along its length. The tunnel ended at the bottom of a natural basin, its sloping walls covered in ferns and saplings. Christina sat at the top of the basin wall, huddled under a tree for shelter.

'The view's even better from here!' she shouted.

Hector pulled himself to his feet and made for the nearest sapling. He hoisted himself up the trunk to gain a foothold on the rim of the basin. Like Christina, his head was up amongst the lowest branches of a huge bean tree. He squirmed as a large drop of water, disturbed from the leaves above, ran down his back.

'Hey, Lil, you should see the view from up here. It's like being on top of the trees.'

'Yeah, you look like a monkey too.'

Hector looked down and saw Lily's head emerge from the small tunnel. He wondered if she'd make it all the way through, or if her arse would get stuck.

'Shit, this wall scratches,' she said as she pulled herself clear and stood up. She rubbed at her left shoulder and noticed the rip that had appeared in her T-shirt. 'Bastard,' she hissed, spitting into the mossy ground.

'I bet the marines had meetings here,' Christina said.

Lily gave her a blank look. 'Maybe,' she said.

'I think they all got pissed here and fell asleep,' Hector said.

Lily blinked up at him through the raindrops. 'You know you sound like your grandfather—all this war stuff.'

'Well, don't you ever think about it?' he said. He didn't want to look at her. She was taunting him, the bitch.

'No,' she said, 'at least I never used to.' Her voice dropped and was hard to hear over the spattering rain. She mumbled something about the sword.

Hector let go of the tree and dropped to the floor of the basin beside her.

'What did you say?' he said.

'I said I've only started thinking about it since we found the sword.' She looked away from him, back towards the small entrance hole. 'I don't like it, Hector. I don't want to think about it at all.'

Hector felt helpless. He wanted to comfort her, tell her it was OK, but nothing came out of his mouth. He watched her kneel down, ready to crawl back into the tunnel.

'I'm going back, it's creepy up here,' she said. 'Come on, Christina.'

Christina slid back down to the tunnel entrance. She followed Lily out the tight exit.

Hector shrugged off a feeling of unease. He looked around the basin one last time. Something dull brown and smooth caught his eye a third of the way up the mossy wall to his right. He reached out and pulled at the half-buried object. It was another bottle just like the one Lily had found, but this one wasn't damaged. Hector was pleased with his find. He would take it back to Ibu. Then the old man would feel that he had been part of the exploration. He tried to wipe off the black soil and moss. He peered inside the neck and saw nothing but filth.

'I wonder who drank from you, long ago?' he whispered into the neck.

A breeze picked up, swirling around the basin like a tiny wind funnel. It seemed to whisper in answer to his question. '*Egirow, Egirow,*' he thought it said. He shuddered as a tremor ran down his spine.

fifteen

Baringa District
6 March 1943

Alarmed, Tepu let himself slide backwards. Dirt and stones flew down on him; rocks tore at his skin. He fell with a slap against a small ledge, but he did not cry out. Ignoring the pain in his hip, he pulled himself in against the cliff face and cradled his head in his hands.

Above him the Japanese hurried to the edge of the cliff. Revolver shots rang out in the darkness. Some whistled past Tepu and ricocheted off the rocks. He heard marines calling out, shouting orders at one another. Within moments a strong beam of light swept over the drop and the shooting ceased.

Tepu prayed to his ancestors that he wouldn't be found. But where was Tarema? Had he been shot in that first spray of wild gunfire? Tepu berated himself for bringing him here. He should have tried harder to stop Tarema.

There was a flutter of wings. Brushing past Tepu, they

ascended the cliff accompanied by shrill chirruping. Tepu dared not look up but he knew they were black noddies, swooping around the cliff face distracting the marines.

The searchlight withdrew and the voices returned to the familiar tones of laughter and banter.

Tepu lay there for what seemed like hours. When he could no longer hear the Japanese, he extracted himself from his hiding place. He felt his way back down the cliff. Each time he extended his leg to the right he grimaced from the pain in his hip.

Tepu estimated he was near the end of his descent when he heard someone breathing. He pressed himself against the cliff and listened carefully. There it was again, close by to the left. Whoever it was, they were hidden by the scrub that grew at the base of the cliff.

Tepu's veins pulsed with fear. Was it Tarema, lying half dead on the slope? Or was it a marine, waiting to ambush him. If it were Tarema, Tepu's indecision could mean death. If it were a marine, however, surely he would have fired by now.

Tepu crawled towards the sound and whispered Tarema's name.

'You made it at last,' groaned his brother.

'Are you all right? Can you walk?' Tepu said, groping towards him.

Tarema lay inert, covered in rubble. 'I think my ribs are broken. When I breathe it hurts. I wanted to go home but I was worried they'd shot you. I decided to lie here until dawn so I could see what happened to you.'

Tepu gripped his brother's arm affectionately. 'Well

we're both alive. The black noddies saved us. The Japs thought it was only birds making a commotion.'

Again the noddies had come to Tepu's aid. He felt the black stone against his thigh. He was certain the stone was protecting him, keeping him alive for a special purpose. Though what that purpose was, he still wasn't sure.

Ring Road
Wednesday 30 June 2004

The rain had stopped and Lorelei wiped the seat of her scooter with the hem of her skirt. She sat heavily on the cushioned seat, balanced a plastic bag of groceries on the floor, and turned the ignition. The scooter lurched forward and she weaved it through the supermarket carpark, dodging potholes filled with brown water.

She turned to the right, onto the open road and headed for home via Yamek and Baringa Bay. Little clouds of steam floated up from the slick black bitumen before her. There was no traffic on the road. Lorelei liked the northern part of the island because there were so few houses and the road was more scenic. She loved the rise up to Yamek and the view from the top of the hill down into Baringa Bay. The waves crashing against the pinnacles in the bay sparkled in the sunlight and the breeze was soothing against her face.

Sometimes, on days like today and paydays, her surroundings became animated. The pinnacles looked like black giants emerging from the reef; the coconut palms stood in clusters like tall thin ladies bowing to one another and whispering. When Lorelei was a child, her family came out to the bay and went swimming or collected shellfish on the reef.

They often went to Baringa Bay or further around to Leper Beach, where Aunt Edouwe had once lived. Lorelei's mother, Rita, had no memory of Edouwe, her eldest sister. Rita was only six months old when the Japanese rounded up her mother and three other siblings and shipped them north to Truk in the Caroline Islands. That was during the war, when the fighting was at its worst. They spent more than two years on Truk in crowded conditions with little to eat, but at least they were with other Tevuans.

Rita was still a small child when she returned to Tevua. No one told her much about her sister Edouwe or her grandparents—people just said they died, drowned somehow. But a lot of people died during the war, even Rita's mother and one of her brothers. They were buried in Truk. Rita and her two surviving sisters were reunited with their father. He had been forced to work for the Japanese. They never talked about the war. The family losses were too great and too painful. Well that's what Rita and her sisters had always said.

As a child Lorelei would wade along the reef with her mother and aunties. They would hunt amongst the shallow water for tasty *ebon* and octopus. If they found anything delicious Rita would prise the seafood from the rocks, put it in a small basin and give thanks to God. Then she would say a silent prayer over the reef in the direction of Leper Beach. It was for their lost Aunt Edouwe, Rita would say.

Lorelei even suspected her mother cried as she prayed, but she always wiped her wet hands across her face and Lorelei never knew if it was tears or sea water.

The sad moments were brief because Eldon would always be with them, still too young to go out with the men and their nets. He never failed to find a velvet black sea slug, force it to disembowel itself, then throw it at his sisters. Gertrude and Eide wouldn't flinch, but Lorelei ran screaming up the beach hounded by the laughter of her siblings. She had hated sea slugs ever since.

Just past the Baringa restaurant Lorelei turned her head and caught sight of movement near the old car wrecks. Teenagers hanging around as usual.

Lily? Was that her? What was she doing there with that white girl and that brat of a kid, Hector? They were at the jeep though, must be with his crazy grandfather. Lorelei had half a mind to turn back but thought better of it. She'd deal with Lily when they were at home, she'd make her see reason. The stupid girl thought she wouldn't be spotted eh? Shit girl, what does she think she's doing, going round with that thief? You can't wander around with a boy in broad daylight, what would people think? They'd all call you a *trut*. Why, oh why didn't Lily stay home and study? Why did she always go off on her own and skip school? She was never home. Lorelei's mouth twisted. She was pissed off now. Such a short burst of happiness and now Lily had gone and spoilt it all.

At home, she bolted down a few beers and waited for Lily to return. No one else was home. She played patience and smoked while she waited, looking up all the time at the wall clock. Lorelei had always admired the clock, one of her most prized possessions. The love heart shape was rimmed with a thick gold casing, so beautiful and shiny. It was a pity it hung against the wall smeared with mould. Lorelei fancied she was a bit like the clock: bright and special, in tatty surroundings.

Time dawdled and still Lily hadn't returned. The sound of a car pulling up out the front jolted Lorelei back to the present. A horn tooted.

'Lorelei! You there?' came Daphne's voice.

Lorelei waddled over to the kitchen door and made her way outside. A rusty sedan idled under the fig tree. The driver was Eide's sister-in-law, Ruby, and in the back sat Lily and the white girl.

Daphne called to her from the passenger seat, 'You coming with us? Eide's real sick. She's flying out tomorrow. We're going to the hospital to see her now.' She gestured to the back seat, 'We've got Lil with us.'

All her fury drained at the sight of them. There was no way she was going to tell her daughter off now, not with her sister so sick and hospital visits on everyone's mind. Lily had fooled her again. Lorelei snorted and wiped at her face.

sixteen

Yamek District
11 March 1943

A Tevuan Elder visited the camp one evening just as the air cooled and the sun was low in the sky.

'The Tevuan Chief has given instructions,' he said, 'all girls of marriageable age in Tevua must get married. It's his plan, to make sure girls are protected, that they each have a man providing for them.'

'How will they marry when we must keep to the curfew and there is so little food?' one of the camp residents asked.

'There will be no feast. If couples are willing, then the boy will go and stay with her at her home. The union will be recognised. Every girl who has reached womanhood is encouraged to find a husband.'

What about Edouwe? thought Tepu. She must have been his age or older. She would be forced to marry. If only she would marry him, Tepu, and not some other boy. The idea of her with someone else made his stomach knot. No, *he* would ask Edouwe. But how would he find time alone with her? Even before the war, custom demanded a chaperone. He needed to gauge her feelings. If she refused his offer he would surely die inside. But if he didn't move quickly, he would probably miss out.

Tevua International Airport
Mawendo District
Thursday 1 July 2004

'What time's the flight?' Amos asked Lily.

They sat together in the parked Landrover waiting for Decima and her family to arrive. They'd left Lorelei sleeping at home. She'd been up all night at the hospital with her sister, Eide, so that the rest of the family could get some sleep before the flight out.

Amos sat behind the steering wheel with a can of beer lodged between his fat thighs and a cloud of cigarette smoke wafting about his face.

'I think it leaves at one o'clock,' Lily said. She wished it wasn't going at all. Lily hated the airport. It was one of the hottest places on the island because the tarmac reflected the morning glare back into the atmosphere. By midday the heat stole your every breath and tears of sweat rolled down your face. But worse than that were the goodbyes. A lot of people never came back, especially teachers and sick relatives.

She wished her mother would fly away forever. She wished it were Lorelei, half dead on the aeroplane, flying to Melbourne. The stupid bitch thought she loved Hector.

Dumb shit Hector, as if she would run off into the forest and screw him! As if she would screw anyone. Except maybe one day. One day she might. Her thoughts drifted to Jonah.

Jonah, Jonah, Jonah—would he be there today? She couldn't think straight. Too much was going through her mind: Jonah's invitation, her mother's threats, Decima going away, Eldon always hanging around the house, and the ghost. Don't leave me, Decima, she thought. How can I be safe without you? She shifted in the seat, trying to get comfortable, but the heat and anxiety made her feel sick.

'It's too hot in here,' she said, opening the door of the Landrover with a creak. 'I'm going over to the departure lounge.'

Amos snorted and opened his door as well. 'I'll be over at The Jade Horse,' he said pointing to the nearest restaurant. 'Come and get me when you're ready to go home.'

Lily dropped from the Landrover and scuffed over to the shade outside the lounge area. She slid her purple hand into the small of her back and leant against the wall. The red bricks were cool against her arms.

Within minutes a parade of passengers walked past. Chinese men with enormous matching suitcases rushed through the doors. An old European man in a suit hobbled along, raking his fingers through his thin yellowed hair. His sharp nose looked lumpy and raw from the sun. Some barefooted Gilbertese women padded past, wearing smocking blouses and colourful *lava lavas*. Strands of black hair, which refused to be pulled back neatly, framed their chiselled features. A Chinese woman and her baby followed. No arse—why did some women have no arse?

Eventually a green sedan pulled into the front carpark. As Decima's family tumbled out, Lily wandered over to help. She picked up the nearest striped canvas bag and lugged it towards the airport doors while Decima babbled away in her ear.

'I can't wait to go. The last time I went to Australia I was ten. I bet it's different now.'

'I don't want you to go,' said Lily.

'I know, but don't worry, I'll bring you back a present. Something special, something blue. You still like blue, don't you?'

'Or some magazines,' Lily said, thinking of her special blue box. There were always pictures of hands in magazines: hands with rings, hands holding drinks, hands of celebrities, beautiful hands. Lily smiled and nudged her friend.

Decima's younger sisters brushed past them, racing for the air-conditioned haven of the check-in area. They were both dressed in brand new clothes and looked so clean their skin almost shone.

'Where's your mum?' Lily asked Decima.

'They're bringing her from the hospital by ambulance.'

'Is she any better?'

Decima looked at her impassively. 'I think, I hope…'

'She'll be fine. You'll be with her.' Lily's voice sounded flat and she wished she hadn't asked. She sighed and squeezed Decima's hand.

Decima tried to smile but Lily sensed she would cry instead. She let her walk off towards the check-in counter.

Later, as they sat together waiting for the boarding call, private fears overwhelmed them both. Lily had no idea how to comfort her friend; she had no words to say but empty ones. They hugged their goodbyes at the departure doors gave each other a feeble high-five. They both knew they mustn't cry.

After the plane faded into the sky, Lily walked up the steps onto the balcony at The Jade Horse. It was the best Chinese restaurant on the island because it had air conditioning, toilets, décor, music and, best of all from Amos's point of view, beer. The balcony was a shady oasis that filtered out the harsh rays from the runway. Lily hesitated while her eyes adjusted to the shadows. Sweat trickled down her neck and the back of her knees.

Amos was drinking with a couple of friends. Some plastic meal containers and a big plate of half-eaten rice littered the table in front of them. As Lily came closer she saw a fly crawling on the remnants of the mound of rice. Amos brushed it away. They still hadn't noticed her. Dumb drunk bastards.

'*Neko*,' Amos called to the young Gilbertese waitress.

A thin girl with a toothy smile approached warily and stayed just out of arm's reach from the men. She held a pencil and pad as her defence: to stab customers and shield herself from their advances.

'More beer,' Amos said, lunging to grope her hips. She saw the move coming and expertly sidestepped.

Unbalanced, Amos teetered on the edge of the seat and flung out his arms to steady himself. One arm landed in the leftover rice. His friends howled with laughter. The waitress rolled her eyes in disgust.

Lily shook her head and approached.

'The plane's gone, Dad. Can we go home?'

He looked up at her with surprise and made an effort to appear sober. 'Ah, Lily, my girl,' he said in a serious tone, picking rice from his forearm with his stubby fingers. 'Not yet, not yet. You see I've just met my old friends here and we're drinking together.'

'Home, don't go home. Come and join us,' one of the friends said with a sleazy glint in his eye.

Lily stood self-consciously in the shadows. The stupid arseholes were like pigs wallowing in mud. She didn't want to go near their party. She kept the same distance the waitress did and choked back her distaste. Still, his drunkenness would suit her plan perfectly. Now she could simply walk to the end of the runway and meet Jonah. She hoped she wouldn't be too early or too late.

'Don't worry, Dad, I'll get a ride home later,' she said. She walked out into the glare of the airport carpark once again, away from their drunken guffawing.

seventeen

Yamek District
26 March 1943

Tepu and Tarema woke to the hum of US bombers and the thudding of blasts in the south of the island. Again they were targeting the runway. The brothers scrambled round the edge of the camp to see what was happening. The black sky filled with streaming coloured lights. With each blast an orange glow expanded on the horizon and Tepu imagined another Jap plane exploding into flames. Flashes of red trailed upwards as the Japanese guns answered and the battle continued into the night.

'The Americans must win. The bombs will blow the Japs off our island!' exclaimed Tarema.

'We should go back and stay with mother in case the planes drop bombs close by,' said Tepu. He wished this was the night when the Japs were all killed and there would be no more digging, no more bowing and no more hunger.

But the next day the marines came once more and escorted Tepu and the other men back to work.

She's here, Hector observed. My girl, Lily. Still hanging off that jerk Jonah. Why did the girls like him? There must be something about football players. If you're strong enough to play football, then you get the girls. If you're a skinny little runt with a busted face, no one wants to know you.

Football sucked. It was a stupid game. Besides, it was too hot to run around an oval of crushed coral when the sun grilled the island. Those guys wanted to turn black. They probably thought if they were black their dicks would get bigger, like those black guys on the X-rated movies.

Volleyball was a better game. For a start no one wanted to punch your head in, and you didn't have to stay out there for hours at a time. Plus there was always shell on the team, plenty of girls to look at.

Hector had scored a place on the Dragons team today. They were sitting out this game, having lost the previous one to the Sharks. So the Sharks played on and the biggest shark of all was pretty-boy Jonah, who was showing off on the court in front of Lily.

Hector sat by the net on the sideline trying to give Jonah the evil eye. He had to make sure the Sharks lost. That would be sweet justice. He hoped Jonah would go back to Pago in his so cool Bob Marley T-shirt and shades, and step in dog shit on the way. Arsehole.

Lily wandered over towards Hector and sat beside him. He felt the blood rush to his cheeks and he didn't know where to look.

'How are the chickens?' she said.

'Taste good. What's happening?' he asked.

'I just saw Decima off. She's gone to Melbourne. I thought I'd come here to look for some fun,' she said.

'What kind of fun?' he asked winking at her.

'*Suh!*' she scolded him.

'There's no fun in Tevua, you know that,' he said.

She smiled but looked away quickly. He saw her gaze fall on Jonah. Lily was out to catch her own shark, Mr pretty-boy from Pago.

'Hope Sharks lose,' he said.

'They won't,' she said, her eyes on Jonah. He was serving now, holding the ball in one hand, as if it were merely a cushion. He spat to one side as he prepared himself for the big bash.

Bounce, bounce, bounce—Jonah was almost ready now.

Hector spat into the grey sand. Jonah the arsehole thought he was so cool, didn't he?

Jonah threw the ball and leapt into the air just as Hector blew the loudest raspberry he could. The distraction didn't faze Jonah and he slammed the ball over the net.

Hector felt Lily turn towards him. She must have been giving him that 'stupid shit' glare, but he was too ashamed to turn to her. He searched in his pocket, pulled out an Oxo cube and unwrapped it.

'Do you want to go up to the bunker again?' he said, picking at the cube and offering her some at the same time.

'No,' she said, looking away.

'We could go up to Government Settlement again, find something else.'

Now Lily faced him. 'Mum doesn't like me being with you. She gets mad.'

'And what about you? Do you like hanging around me?'

'*Suh!*' she shouted at him and pushed him so hard he fell back and his head hit the concrete with a thud. He blinked back the pain and righted himself. She laughed at him, so he swore back at her. He was enjoying this— obviously she didn't mind his company at all, otherwise she would have walked away.

Hector looked at her honey-brown skin for a long time, noting again the scars on her legs. He knew she was tough, just like most Tevuan girls, but he wondered exactly what happened when Lorelei lost her temper.

'My parents used to get mad, too,' he said. 'Ibu's good though, he doesn't hit me.'

'He couldn't catch you,' Lily said, laughing.

'That's right.' He flicked a small stone into the air and watched it fall at the feet of one of the volleyballers. 'What have you done with the sword?' he asked.

Lily stared at him. 'It's at home. It's hidden.'

'What are you going to do with it, cut toddy?'

They both laughed, imagining someone climbing a coconut tree with the sword. How stupid.

'It keeps me safe,' she said. Then in a whisper she added, 'Or it will—something like that.'

eighteen

Tepu's legs shook, ready to run. His mind was alert for any danger. He knew they had to work quickly. Once the shock of the blast had faded, Tarema grabbed a woven-coconut basket and pulled him down to the beach. In the light of dawn the water was a transparent wash that rippled and shimmered, hiding the subtle contours of the reef. On top of the pale moving surface floated dozens of dark shapes. The boys stumbled in their efforts to collect as many of the stunned fish as the basket could hold.

A shout from the beach made them turn. More people from the camp were coming, once they knew that the Americans' wayward bombs had delivered a bounty from the sea. Hungry children in rags scampered onto the reef, scooped up fish and sunk their teeth into them. The women from the camp scurried towards the children berating them for their greed.

Tepu and Tarema hauled their catch onto the beach. With sea water streaming from their shorts, they ran home to the lean-to, making certain not a single fish fell.

Their mother greeted them with haunted eyes.

'It's a feast, Mother!' Tarema shouted, passing her a fish.

'You go ahead, eat,' she said.

'There's plenty for all of us. And we ate yesterday while you went without.'

She sniffed at the food and took a small bite. 'You boys need your strength,' she said. 'It's wasted on me.'

Tepu was horrified at her words. 'No, don't say that, you must eat. We all must.'

'What is the use? We'll all rot here in the next few months. If the bombs don't kill us, then the Japanese will. There's nothing to live for.'

The brothers exchanged worried glances.

'You can't think like that, Mother. It will end soon. The Americans will save us. I know they will,' Tarema said.

Tepu sat brooding. He was distressed by his mother's words and by his inability to provide more food than the meagre rations from the marines.

'We have to do something,' he told Tarema later that day. 'She sickens because she is weak.' He rocked his head in his hands. 'What can I do?'

'I'll get more food,' his brother said, 'even if we have to keep eating lizards. I'll find more.'

'You style, Jonah,' Lily said.

He wandered over to her, his T-shirt dripping with sweat. It clung to his body, highlighting his muscles.

'*Suh!*' he laughed.

'I've been watching. You're a mean spiker.'

'I need longer legs,' he said, spilling a bottle of water over his short black hair. He shook the drips off then upended the bottle to drink the dregs.

'What do you mean?' said Lily.

'Those tall boys are good for spiking. Not me.' He indicated two of his team-mates who were wandering off towards the Ring Road.

Lily clutched one of the volleyball posts and leant against it. 'Eh, you do fine,' she said. She was desperate to say something more, to keep the conversation moving. She needed to keep him there with her, but her mind was blank.

Behind him she could see some of his family approaching. This was the end of their meeting.

'Come on, we're going,' said his brother. He was a smaller but older and fatter version of Jonah. He greeted Lily by raising his eyebrows.

'What are you doing now?' Jonah asked Lily.

Surprised, she couldn't think of a quick answer. 'Nothing special,' she blurted.

'We're going round the island. Want to come?' Jonah said.

Lily hesitated. It wasn't right: you just didn't get into

a car with a bunch of boys, and you certainly didn't go round with people you only vaguely knew. You just didn't do it because you didn't know what was on their minds. Still, she figured she'd never get closer to Jonah's world than she was now unless she took a few risks.

'Yeah, why not.'

Jonah looked to his brother who raised his eyebrows again. 'We'll drop her at Anbwido,' the brother said.

'No!' she said. 'At Baringa Channel.' God, what would her mum say if she saw her getting dropped off by a car full of boys? What would anyone say for that matter, her dad, Rongo? Oh just think of it, shit!

Jonah's brother looked at her with amusement. 'OK. Want to go swimming?'

'Eh, no,' she said. There was something about him she didn't like. Was he mocking her? He was too smooth, too cool for her in his pressed island shirt and wraparound sunglasses.

The back seat of the sedan smelled of cigarette smoke and vinyl interior. Lily eased her way over to the far end against the door. The door handle was missing but at least there was a lever for the window.

Jonah and his cousin, Roy, pushed in after her. Another of Jonah's cousins, fat and giddy on his feet, hauled himself into the front passenger seat. Oh-so-cool big brother sat in the driver's seat with his sunglasses tilted at just the right angle so you could see his eyebrows. He looked at the three of them all squashed in the back. 'Now you behave yourselves. We're going to get some beer.'

Beer! Lily felt herself scream inside. She was desperate to get out, but she dared not speak. She knew this was a big mistake, but they had begun to drive off, heading around the island on their way to a sly grog shop.

'Want a smoke, Lil?' Jonah asked as he took the gold packet from the compartment between the front seats.

'Nah,' she said, hoping she didn't sound like a little kid. She tried not to appear nervous, but it was hard to relax. She didn't want to press up too tightly while Roy was sitting on the other side, but she couldn't escape the fact that her thigh brushed against Jonah's. And Jonah didn't seem to mind. He turned to her as he lit his cigarette and winked.

Lily sighed and some of the fear and tension left with her breath. She could tell Jonah was showing off and he really did want her to be there with him. She knew she'd be all right. She felt happy for once, happier than she'd been for months.

As she gazed out the window she could smell the rotting sea life from the reef and the breeze off the waves flicked in her face. She smiled to herself as they passed the old tin sheds that made up Chinatown. A few cars were parked in the gravel out the front and she could see coloured blow-up toys hanging in the doorways. Lily always loved shopping in Chinatown. She was fascinated by the hundreds of products packed into such little stores. Boxes and boxes of T-shirts and shorts, piles of towels and racks of lacy, frilled satin dresses for preschool girls. All packed in tightly, just like her in the back seat of the car.

She tensed for just an instant as she felt Jonah touching her right hand, pulling it down onto the seat between their thighs. She shot him a quick glance, frightened that Roy would see, but Jonah simply winked at her again, while Roy untangled a cassette tape and argued with the two in the front about last week's football match.

Jonah's hand was strong and smooth in hers and his touch sent a buzz of warmth up her arm, filling her chest with a growing tightness that dulled everything else around her. She knew it now—he did like her. He liked her a lot. But he was holding her good hand, not her purple one. She slipped her left hand under her thigh.

The jolt of the car turning off the road brought her back to reality. It rolled over huge potholes, scraped its exhaust and came to rest a little way from the front of a large white house.

Big brother and drunk cousin lurched out into the yard towards the shaded entrance at the side. Roy opened his door to follow them.

'Don't you two do anything naughty now,' he laughed as he walked away. Jonah squeezed her hand tightly. Together they watched Roy enter at the side door. He didn't look back.

Jonah looked at her sideways. 'No one can see us,' he said, sinking low, level with her breasts. 'Come here,' he whispered, pulling her down, 'I want to kiss you.'

Lily had no time to react. He pressed against her, breathing cigarette breath all over her lips as he kissed her. She flinched, tasting the sharp scent of tobacco, but his lips and tongue were soft against hers. His body was warm and strong and she began to melt as he pulled her closer. She was surprised at how smooth his face was, not rough and scratchy like Eldon.

She froze. No! Why did she think that? How could she think that? She wanted to enjoy this moment, but fear took over. Jonah's tongue pushed inside her mouth, wet and probing. She felt crushed in the confines of the back seat. She pushed him away, her breath coming short and frightened. They'd be found out, she knew they would.

'No, not here, not now. I'm scared,' she whispered.

He moved away from her and laughed. She looked up at him; he seemed different. She could now see a kind of roughness about his skin, pimples she'd never really noticed before. He certainly wasn't as slick as his older brother, but he wasn't as fat either. She liked his leanness and the gap between his teeth.

'When then?' he said.

Lily righted herself against the door and glanced towards the house. She struggled for an answer but nothing would come. She was so excited that she felt an electric buzz run through her again. Her mouth opened and shut like a newly landed fish but her brain was empty.

The three men emerged into the sunlight from the side of the house.

'Shit, they're coming,' she turned back to Jonah. 'Tomorrow after midday, at Baringa Channel,' she said.

He grinned. 'What is it with you and the channel?'

Alone at Baringa, Lily watched Jonah's car drive away, black smoke billowing off to the side as it accelerated.

Once it disappeared she ran alongside the road then down the track that led to Leper Beach. She'd have to be careful along the casino beach. But she wouldn't be spotted now in the dusk. No one looked seaward at night. They were all too busy with the road and who was on it—going round.

She raised her fists in triumph. '*Aue!*' she shrieked, flinging her head back to laugh at the sky. 'He likes me!' Hearing the whooping ring of her voice hang in the air, she stopped. She didn't want everyone at the casino to hear. But she couldn't stop grinning. He kissed me! I'm special. I'm really someone, now!

The high grass opened into a clearing. A few more strides and she was underneath the beach almonds on the shore. Pinnacles loomed up on the right, huge shadows against the curtain of dusk. The tide was coming in. She was cut off from her walk around the hotel. Never mind, once darkness came she would make her way through the casino grounds without anyone seeing her.

She sat on the sand and peered out to sea. 'Without anyone seeing her', what a weird thing to think. No one ever really *saw* her. Enough people looked at her, she knew that. But how many people really saw her for what she was? Just a couple: Decima, maybe Hector. She laughed, thinking about him, that skinny brat, and how her mum thought they were together. As if she'd ever kiss that busted face, huh! But now, now Jonah had touched her and she was certain Jonah really saw her. He noticed her, he kissed her. Yeesss! He liked her. Liked her enough to see her again tomorrow. And then, what would they do?

She sat daydreaming about Jonah's embrace. The darkening colours formed large shapes about her. A whisper on the breeze sang a tune she knew: a faint whine that she remembered from her dreams. The sound grew till it became the same wailing noise that haunted her so many times as she woke. '*Egirow, Egirow*,' it seemed to say. Why did the sea call out 'angry'? And why had her birthmark begun to burn once more? She shivered and rubbed her arm, wondering if she was going crazy.

In the twilight the nearest pinnacle seemed to sway. It became the image of a woman in rags who shimmered before her, then was gone. Startled, she glanced about. The hairs on her arms and neck prickled and she could feel her heart thudding against her chest. Now she wasn't only hearing things, she was seeing things too—another ghost. Was she really going crazy? Crazy like Riki. He could see ghosts. Surely it was only her eyes fooling her in the fading light.

Around her the dusk had vanished and she was suddenly aware of the darkness. Lily jumped up from the sand and walked back to the clearing, past the tennis courts, then down the steps that led to the hotel carpark. She hovered at the base of the steps for a moment, gauging how far off the next headlights were as they swung into the hotel driveway. Satisfied she could make it, she dashed into the garden at the side of the carpark.

She sank into the protection of the greenery as the headlights flooded the garden around her. She dared not look but she could tell by the voices shouting above the engine that the car was full of drunken men. The engine was cut and the lights died. Car doors opened and slammed shut. There was a huge eruption of guffawing and a thud against the body of the car.

'Stand up, ya bastard. I can't carry you to the bar,' someone said.

'You go, I'll be there soon,' said another voice.

Lily heard the scuffing of the men's thongs as they walked heavily towards the hotel. Then she heard another sound: the heavy breathing of a man approaching. She stiffened, trying not to breathe. He was so close she could smell his beer breath and sweat. Did he know she was there, hunched over in the bushes, too frightened even to look?

Lily heard the sprinkle on the leaves before she felt the warm wet spray hit her legs. She wanted to cry out in anger, but she just knelt there, huddled in the bushes, paralysed, and did nothing.

Always do nothing! What's wrong with you girl? She felt the indignity of it all churn inside her but she did nothing except hold her breath and wait.

As soon as the drunk had staggered off towards the hotel Lily got to her feet and ran on through the garden, across the driveway and down over the embankment to the sea. She strode into the waves as they swept up the beach, hoping the salt water would wash away her disgust. Stupid arseholes, stupid bastards, she thought. They'll get it one day.

Back at the house, she could tell from the darkness of the building, the muted sounds and the flickering light from the DVD player, that she had to be wary. And all those cars and bikes were in the driveway. The house was full of men.

She edged up to the side of the building, held her breath and peeked through the crack in the curtain. She could just make out the scene inside the darkened room where several boys lay on their stomachs with their eyes fixed on the screen. One was Cyrus, others were young kids from around Anbwido, some as young as five years old.

The movie flashed to a new camera angle. Every DVD seemed to show the same white sluts. Always heaps of white sluts, they must love it. One slut with two or three guys, pump, pump, pump. Lily felt the pit of her abdomen tickle with fascination. Repulsed by her reaction, she forced her eyes away to inspect the audience again.

It was hard to see the entire room through her spy hole. Rongo and Joachim were there sipping beers, and Mitchell, one of Decima's older brothers, sat on the floor. 'Give me a smoke,' came Eldon's voice, directly below Lily's peeping hole.

She moved back with a start then tiptoed away from the house, just as laughter rang out from inside.

Dazed and miserable, Lily walked back to the beach. Where now? Where tonight? She stumbled onto the sand, kicking an empty corned beef can into the blackness of the reef. Its clatter was drowned out by the roll of the waves. Take it away, sea, take all the rubbish away. She wished it would take her rubbish family away.

The pillbox would be empty; she could go and wait

there. Then she remembered the ghost and hesitated, looking back to the house. The boys would soon disperse, especially when they heard Lorelei arriving home after bingo. Still, the threat at home from Eldon was real and maybe the ghost wasn't. Perhaps it was just a one-off thing that would disappear. Eldon wouldn't fade. He never went away. She started walking to the pillbox.

She saw the concrete dome, pale in the night, as she rounded the bend of the beach. Bushes and tall grass screened it from the road.

Leaning against the pillbox she felt the radiant warmth of the concrete. She hauled herself up and perched on the roof, hugging her knees to her chest. Here there was peace. The smell of urine and rotting sea life was all around her, but it wasn't foul enough to make her turn back. Nothing would make her go home now to drunken men and X-rated movies.

As she listened to her breath and the sound of the waves she lay back on the concrete and let the trapped warmth seep into her spine. She could hear the boom, boom, boom of old Landrovers passing on the road. Their lights caught the scrub beside her and voices screeched over the heavy thud of the bass.

The sky was indigo like the eye of a tuna and the stars were small white points. Lily gazed into the night, smiling to herself with the memory of Jonah's kiss, the warmth of his hands, the taste of his lips.

A light blinked in the sky just where her eyes were focused; a plane must be coming in. The blinking alternated red and white, and the intensity grew. As Lily watched the lights, a gust chilled her skin. The cold chased away her warm memories. She shivered. A prickling fear grew in her gut. She sensed someone watching her. Startled, she turned and saw a figure standing beside the pillbox. It was the *yani,* the ghost of the marine.

'Suh!' she shouted and sprang up, terrified he would touch her. She scrambled to her feet and instantly felt the energy drain from her body.

'Go away! Leave me!' she screamed.

The *yani* came no closer. He stood and mouthed at her. Mouthed what Lily thought must have been orders. That's what they did in the war, they shouted orders at people. That's what Riki had said.

She sucked in her breath, felt the chilled air fill her lungs. She had to be brave, she had to do something. 'What do you want?' she shouted.

The *yani* motioned at her roughly with his right hand in a fist, holding it above his head as if he were punching the air in victory, but his face was grim and furious.

Lily inched away, aware that in some way he was threatening her, but as she moved the image faded and the breeze dropped. She was alone again on the pillbox and the roar of the descending jet overhead rumbled her bones.

She breathed deeply, feeling her heart thump. She clutched at her stained hand. It was burning again, a fierce tingling sensation. Why did it hurt each time she saw the ghost? Riki had said her birthmark was special, but right now she feared it and she feared what was happening to her. This must be how it is when you go crazy, she thought. And why was a ghost from World War Two haunting *her*? She had nothing to do with the war, except for finding the sword. That was it—she had a Japanese sword. It must have belonged to the *yani* and now he wanted it back. So he was haunting her. Well, it was hers now, and he could piss off. She wasn't going to get rid of it.

Taking another deep breath, she tried to compose herself. The tension in her legs willed her to run away but she didn't dare go back home. Instead she jumped down from the pillbox and crawled into the entrance. The stink of beer and urine was overpowering. Gingerly she felt about in the dark for a place to hide. She pushed aside a few rocks and lay with her head in the entrance, her body just inside. As she tried to sleep her mind filled with visions of ghosts and Eldon. She sniffed away her fears. The *yani* might come back, but at least Eldon would never find her here.

nineteen

Tepu was troubled. Night had come and Tarema still hadn't made it home. Should he look for him, or wait a bit longer?

Although she'd said nothing, there was foreboding in his mother's eyes. She was so drained of vigour that anxiety was an emotion she no longer expressed. It took too much energy.

They'd just finished eating a meagre meal, a small rat Tarema had caught early in the day, when they heard footsteps.

'You there, Tepu?' called a young Gilbertese man from the path beside the lean-to.

Tepu rose and greeted him. It was another worker, a youth about the same age as Tepu.

'I'm sorry, friend, to bring bad news. Come quickly, they've caught Tarema and another boy. You must help me bring them home.'

Anbwido
Thursday 1 July 2004

The black ribbon of bitumen ran beneath her wheels. Lorelei had to concentrate hard to keep the scooter from wobbling, especially once she'd geared down. She bumped her way over the kerb into the driveway filled with motorbikes and cars, all belonging to Rongo's friends. If it was a party, they weren't making much noise and the house was dark except for the kitchen light at the back. They probably had a porno showing again. The dumb bastards thought she was at bingo and wouldn't be home until midnight, but she'd been at the casino instead and had run out of money early. It was only ten-thirty. She looked forward to the shock they'd get.

She cut the engine and propped the scooter, nearly tipping sideways herself as she moved towards the house as quietly as possible. They were so stupid if they thought they could hide it from her. She'd show 'em.

As she reached the corner of the building the house suddenly came alive with activity. The light in the lounge flicked on, Joachim called for players for a hand of Chinese poker and someone opened the fridge door. Shit, she wasn't quick enough.

She peered in through the fly-screen door and saw Rongo with an armful of beer cans.

'Where is it?' she hissed at him, trying to keep her voice down.

'What, Mum?'

'Where's the movie you've been watching?'

'Why, you want to watch it? It's just that footy one Dad had.'

She pushed the screen door open and it hit against the wall with a clack. 'You lie, I know what you've been watching, you shit.' She narrowed her eyes at him and her top lip curled in anger.

Rongo shrugged his shoulders. He looked hurt and wide-eyed, just like he had when he was a little boy, and she knew then that he was lying, but he was too big for her to hit now.

'True, Mum, you go ask the boys.'

She barged in and snatched herself a beer.

'Hey Lorelei, where you been?' Joachim called from the table in the lounge room. 'Come and play, we need one more.'

She snorted, but strode over to the spare chair anyway, cracked open her beer and fell into the chair. Who cared about the movie? Now she had a chance to win something, unlike with the poker machines.

'Where's Lil?' she asked Rongo.

'I think she's sleeping,' he said, nodding towards his sister's room.

Joachim's small fat hands shuffled the cards in a blur and he slammed the pack down in front of Lorelei for her to cut.

She cut as she drank from her beer and eyed the dozen boys sitting idly on the floor. 'Put some music on, boys,' she shouted at them, spraying half a mouthful of beer.

They moved instantly. Some disappeared out the kitchen door while Cyrus and three others busied themselves about the tape recorder on the floor.

Lorelei smiled. Even though Rongo, and now Lily, weren't frightened of her, she could still make the smaller ones quake. As Joachim dealt the cards she wiped the spittle from her chin, then picked up her cards and sorted them according to suit.

The boys on the floor got the music going: a country and western tune with a tortured American twang rang clear into the night.

'My D – I – V – O – R – C – E becomes final today...'

'Stop stuffing with the volume, you kids. I like this one, turn it up!' She looked at her hand of cards and her competitive instinct was triggered. The night became a drift of clubs and diamonds, straights and full houses, while the stench of beer and cigarette smoke filled the house and every pore of her body.

It was after four in the morning by the time Rongo's friends left, all except Joachim who had fallen asleep on the lounge room mat.

Lorelei staggered past Lily's room and saw the door was ajar. She leant in the doorway and turned on the light. No one was there. The mattress hadn't even been put down and her mat was still rolled in the corner. Where was she, the bitch? There was no Decima to stay with now. Where the hell was she? Out screwing half the boys on the island, no doubt. Out screwing that runty little busted-faced Gilbertese thief. Shit! A rage built inside her as she imagined the worst.

'*Trut!*' she screamed and shoved the propped mattress in her fury. It wobbled and flopped to the ground revealing a rectangular shape against the wall.

Lorelei caught her breath and teetered at the door, her eyes struggling to focus. Then it was clear, it was a DVD—probably the one she'd been searching for. She reached in and picked it up. There was no label. She was certain it was the porno. And with a pang of guilt she was certain of something else too: she knew why her daughter hadn't wanted to come home to sleep.

twenty

Baringa Bay
18 April 1943

The youth led Tepu south through the forest. Not far from the path leading up to the Baringa Bay bunker two coconut trees stood in a clearing. Tepu saw a dark shape huddled at the base of each one.

'He's over there,' the youth said, pointing to the furthest tree.

Tepu ran and whispered to the slumped figure of his brother. 'I'm here now, I'll take you home.' But no answer came except the soft gurgle and rattle of Tarema's breath. He shook him gently, but still there was no response. Tepu took a deep breath to quell his rage. The smell of blood and urine filled his senses, forcing bile into his mouth. He fought back the urge to vomit.

'Hurry, Tepu!' the youth called from the other side of the clearing, 'the patrols will come again soon.'

Tepu fumbled in the dark and felt the ropes that bound Tarema to the tree. He sawed at them with his knife until they broke. Tarema pitched forward into the sand. Tepu lifted him over his shoulder then staggered to his feet. The marines would pay for this, he swore. There would be blood for blood.

Anbwido
Friday 2 July 2004

Hector made his way up the Witch Track behind Lotus Restaurant. An idea had been troubling him for days, growing in his mind until it was all he thought about. If the sword was half buried in the bush where they'd caught the chicken, what else was up there? Would there be other treasures, other things from the war?

Hector tipped the last drops of a soft drink into his mouth, then tossed his can away into the bushes. He was prepared this time. He'd brought with him one of his longer whittled sticks, sturdy enough to use as a walking stick or to dig with if needed.

Maybe he'd find another bottle. Ibu had liked the bottle, even though it wasn't a weapon. He said it could whisper a story to him if he listened hard enough. That's because bottles had mouths, the old man reasoned, and the drinkers were telling a few stories at the time they drank.

Hector laughed. Imagine if it were true—what would they say, all the crushed VB cans that covered the surface of the island? Or even the can he'd just tossed.

After about five minutes walk he reached the site where they'd found the sword. Dead leaves had already covered the disturbed ground and Hector realised that if he'd left it for another week he would have had trouble finding it again.

He cleared away the leaves with his stick, then dug deeply in the black soil. Small black hopping bugs and tiny crawling insects writhed in the wet humus, desperate for the cover of rotting leaves. He pushed them aside with his free hand and continued to dig around with the stick, exposing white coral shards amongst the black soil and then the grey sand of the deeper layers.

There was nothing but the earth and Hector felt cheated. He was so sure he would find something else. 'Bastard!' he shouted, getting to his feet and flinging his stick into the air. It flew into the scrub behind him and lodged high in the tangle of tree hibiscus that formed a kind of hedge.

Ngaitirre! That was a good stick, he cursed. He shook each of the hibiscus trunks in turn, trying to shift it. Finally it dropped down, but fell on the other side of the hedge. He forced his way between two trunks and bent down to grab it. But in that moment he saw the rounded shape of an eye socket and a smooth skull. Although dark grey and partly buried, it was definitely human.

'Ey!' he shouted, leaping back from the hedge. His breath stuck in his throat. He looked about in terror, expecting a skeleton to jump out from the trees around him, but the forest was still in the dappled light. He gulped back his fear and pushed into the hedge once more. This time he saw that the skull lay at the foot of two pinnacles, completely hidden by the hedge of tree hibiscus. The soil about it had been disturbed by the busy claws of wild chickens and Hector noted that, even though only a small section of the upper jaw was visible, a few teeth remained.

He picked up his stick and backed away, unable to take his gaze from the gaping eye. He stumbled over the earth he'd disturbed. It had only been a few steps, so close that Hector realised it was probably the sword's owner he'd found.

He shuddered, thinking of the sword and how Lily had been haunted. Would the ghost come after him now? His chest burst with adrenaline and before he even realised it, he was racing through the forest back to the Witch Track.

twenty-one

In the early morning of the second day Tarema stopped breathing.

For the first time since the Japanese invaded, Tepu cried. No matter how he thought about it, he felt responsible for his brother's death. He hadn't kept watch over him, hadn't protected him. His own inability to provide for his family had prompted Tarema to take more risks. Each week his little brother had managed to steal something from the Japanese stores. He stole to keep them alive, Tepu and their mother. But this time he'd been caught.

The struggle against the Japanese seemed futile. Each day they broke the spirit of the islanders, broke it with starvation, violence, death. And now it seemed to Tepu the Japanese had won. He sat hunched by the lean-to, listening to his mother's weeping.

The chatter of a black sea tern startled him. He looked

up. The ancestor bird was perched on one of the pinnacles that formed the wall of the lean-to. Its eyes shone with an eerie green light.

'Use the stone,' the bird rasped. Then it faded from view.

Tepu clutched at the black stone in his pocket. Its warmth radiated up his arm. He would do as the bird said. He would use the stone to avenge his brother and he would plan carefully.

Baringa Bay
Friday 2 July 2004

Lily trudged along the sand towards the channel. Was he there already? Would he be there at all? He probably wouldn't even show up. Her fears churned over and over in her head until she began to feel sick.

The tide was coming in, waves rushed up the wrinkled brown flats of the reef and hurtled themselves at the exposed coral pinnacles. They were like playful children ambushing their petrified grandfathers who gazed out to sea. Some pinnacles were sharp gritty demons, tall and imposing, while others were no more than broken boulders. They stood proudly in the salty stink of rotting sea slugs and the steady creep of green algae. Perhaps the pinnacles were the frozen forms of her ancestors, or drowned souls returning to their homeland. She often imagined that the wailing in her recurring nightmare was actually a pinnacle calling out to her—perhaps her long departed ancestor, Edouwe. What had happened to her?

She'd probably never find out. Her mother and her aunties didn't seem to know much to pass on.

The channel was deserted. Lily walked up to the ramp and saw there were no cars at the parking bay either. She sat on some rocks in the shade of a twisted tree that leant over the beach. She, waited and wondered about Jonah and why he was different from other guys. She loved how confident he was and how he went off on his own and mixed with anyone. She loved the gap between his teeth and the muscles of his arms. She loved the way he touched her, held her, kissed her and she hoped she'd get to experience it again. She hoped yesterday wasn't just a dream, or some kind of ghostly experience like she'd had in the night. She wanted it to be true and real and alive.

'Are you going to swim?' came Jonah's voice, snapping her out of her trance. And there he was, walking down the ramp, so cool in an old blue T-shirt and a pair of black shorts. In all the time she'd been waiting, the tide had come in a long way and most of the reef was under water. Jonah walked straight into the swell. 'Come on!'

She followed him out into the sea, gasping as the water rose about her thighs and then her buttocks, until finally she sank into its depths with only her head bobbing above the waves. Lily reckoned Jonah had gone out to where he could just touch the bottom. She swam out to meet him, then floated on her back beside him, lifting her toes to break the surface.

'I love floating in the waves like this, don't you?' she said.

He grinned at her and she noticed he kept looking at

her chest. She looked down and saw her T-shirt clinging to her breasts.

'Bastard!' she shouted and splashed water at his face.

'Shut up!' he laughed, lunging at her, but she pulled away from him.

'People will see us here,' Lily said.

'You're the one who wanted to meet here.'

'Well let's go into the shallows, so no one can see us from the road.'

He swam over to the side of the channel, then crawled along the reef like a sand hopper in the incoming tide. Lily waded through the shallows wringing out her T-shirt as she went. She slid into the water in front of him where he lay on his belly, propped up on his elbows with his legs pointed out to sea.

She smiled at the admiring pair of eyes in front of her. 'I wondered if you would really come here today. I thought you were joking.'

'I wanted to come. I wanted to see you.'

'You don't seem to want to see me at school,' she said.

'School!' he snorted. 'School's different. We're on holidays now, it's time to play.'

'We play at school too, don't ever do much work. It's just a big waste of time.'

'Yeah, I know, school's crazy, isn't it? But we have to get serious now to do the scholarship exams.'

'So you're Mr Serious at school, are you? Too serious to talk to me?'

'Yeah,' he said, laughing.

'You must like school.'

'No, I hate it. But my dad wants me to sit for the scholarship exam. That's the only reason I go.'

Lily smiled. 'Imagine if you won a scholarship, where would you go?'

'Australia, I guess. My cousin got one a few years ago. He's studying in Melbourne.'

'Bet it's better than Tevua.'

'Yeah.'

A white form brushed past Lily's arm in the swell. She recoiled. '*Suh!* A nappy,' she shouted and tossed the swollen white shape up onto the rocks.

'I thought it had bitten you,' Jonah said.

They both laughed and Lily saw in his eyes that nameless quality that was nervousness and desire, and she grew in strength because of it—he was just as scared as she was. They sat in silence for a while as the waves lapped at them. She wondered what to say next and what was going through his mind.

'Do you believe in ghosts, Jonah?'

'Ghosts?' He looked at her earnestly. 'Yeah...what sort of ghosts?'

'Any kind. Do you see them?'

'No. But my uncle did once.'

'Where?' she asked as she dug her hands into the sand and began to make small hillocks that eroded with each wave.

'You know the story about the giant pig that walks around Yamek? He saw it once, on his way home from a nightclub.'

'Do you believe him?'

'I don't know. I think so. I think there are things out at night, devils and spirits and things we can't know. Have you seen a ghost?'

She took a long time to answer him, wondering whether he'd think she was crazy or not. 'Yeah. I have.'

'You lie.'

His words ate away at her confidence. 'No, not now,' she said softly and she turned her face towards the sea, away from his doubting eyes.

'What kind of ghost?'

She gritted her teeth, wondering whether she should say any more but her words spilled out nervously, 'It's a man, I think he's a soldier…a marine from the war.'

Jonah sat up. His voice was calm and serious. 'Where was it?'

'At the pillbox and near my house. I've seen it twice now. I saw it last night.'

He looked at her, wide-eyed. 'You lie.'

'True, I saw it last night,' she said, but she'd heard the doubt in his voice again. It was all her fault for spoiling the conversation.

'Come on,' he said, standing up, squeezing the water from his shirt. 'It's too hot here, we'll turn black. Let's go to Leper Beach.' He turned to walk away.

'Now?' she said, panic rising in her chest.

He looked back. A smile appeared on his lips. 'Yeah, now,' he said.

twenty-two

Yamek District
24 April 1943

Work had finished for the day and the marines had left Tepu and the other labourers on the border of Yamek and Baringa. The islanders walked as a group down the hill towards the camp.

All the women were gathered on the beach. Many were wailing and comforting one another. Even from the distance of a few hundred feet the men knew something was wrong. They quickened their pace.

'What's happened?' they shouted as they neared the huddled women. But the women saw Tepu, bent their heads and continued weeping.

Tepu's mother was not with them. A feeling of dread surged through him. 'Where's Mother?' he said in a shaky voice.

Nobody spoke but two of the women pointed out to sea. Tepu followed their gaze. The waters were rough, smashing against the reef as if to devour it. Then suddenly all the women spoke at once:

'We were collecting *ebon* on the reef ...'

'We called to her, but she didn't hear us...'

'...just kept walking...'

'...jumped into the sea...'

But one woman's words cut straight at Tepu's heart. 'It was as if she wanted to die.'

He searched the women's stricken faces. Their eyes pleaded with him for forgiveness, as if her suicide was somehow their fault.

Tepu walked away stiffly.

Now he was alone.

Baringa Bay
Friday 2 July 2004

Hector ran onto the Ring Road at the top of the small hill that separated Anbwido from Baringa. Huge tomano trees sheltered him from the sun but still he blinked at the glare of the road. His mind was murky like the water off the reef on a choppy day. He couldn't think far ahead. He didn't know why he'd come this way, instead of going back down to the Lotus Restaurant near Lily's house. He'd gone straight past the path that led down the hill to his home because he didn't want Ibu to see him like this.

He knew he had to tell someone but he wasn't ready yet. He looked down at his hands and saw they were shaking. His chest heaved, his throat burned. He moved across the road and headed for the channel. That's what he needed. A swim would cool him down, clear his mind and stop his body from shaking.

The heat from the afternoon sun drilled into his scalp. He pulled the neck of his T-shirt up over his head to shade him, then jogged down the side of the road towards the channel.

He heard voices below him, laughing. He moved onto the grass and slowed to a walk, breathing deeply to stop his puffing. Then he looked through the low wall of creeper and bushes down onto the beach.

Shit! What was *she* doing here, with *him*? A wave of jealousy swelled within him and he paused, wondering whether to disturb them or not.

Jonah stood up and began to walk through the shallows towards Leper Beach. Lily followed. Hector knew if he didn't stop her now the two of them would be pumping like dogs soon.

'Wait, Lily!' he called out, scrambling over the top of the bushes and down the rocky beachfront.

She looked up at him and shouted, 'Shit! What do you want?'

She's snarling at me, Hector thought.

Jonah looked as though he'd eaten something sour.

Hector ran along the sand, then stopped on the beach in front of them, just out of the water.

'Have you been spying on us?' she said.

'No...'

'*Ngaitirre!*' she cried. 'What are you doing creeping round here?'

'I can come here if I like! You must be doing something

no good if you're so pissed off,' Hector said.

'Bastard! I ought to bust your other eye, you little shit!'

'You couldn't catch me!' he shouted, running back to the rocky embankment.

'Jonah can!' she shrieked, turning to Jonah and pulling at his T-shirt.

But instead of chasing Hector, Jonah grabbed Lily roughly and tripped her up, pushing her over in the water.

'I caught you instead,' he said laughing.

Hector laughed too. Lily's mouth gaped ready to scream and her wet hair clung to her face. She looked ridiculous with all the fury taken out of her.

'Arseholes!' she shouted, then giggled along with them, pulling herself up out of the water.

Hector relaxed on the rocks, confident that he'd spoiled their party and that she wasn't going to murder him. The image of the skull in the forest came back to him and he knew he must tell her about it. He'd have to wait for a better time though, when Jonah wasn't hanging around.

The noise of an old Landrover at the boat ramp made them all turn. Hector recognised it at once as a group of Jonah's neighbours and he smiled to himself. Jonah was trapped now. He couldn't ignore the newcomers and if he stayed with Lily it would be obvious to them what was going on.

'I'll see ya later,' Jonah said quietly to Lily, then he waded through the water to the channel and up the boat ramp where he was immediately offered a can of beer.

Hector jumped down from the rocks and walked to the edge of the water again. 'Come on, Lil. Let's go back.'

'Piss off,' she said coldly.

'But Lil, I've got something to tell you…'

'Just get away, you shit, I don't want to talk to you about anything.' She turned away from him and walked off towards Leper Beach once more.

He followed a few metres behind. 'But Lil, it's about the ghost.'

'Get away!' She stooped, picked up a lump of coral and threw it at him. 'I mean it, piss off and stop following me!'

'I'm not following you.'

'Well, what are you doing right now?' she screamed and he could see her eyes bulging out at him. 'I don't *want* to see you. I don't *want* to talk to you. Just get away, Hector. Just get out of my life!' She hurled another lump of coral at him and then ran off further down the beach.

'You stupid shit!' Hector whispered after her. How was he going to tell her now?

twenty-three

Anbwido District
May 1943

Numb with grief, Tepu toiled each day for the Japanese. The work was an outlet for his pent-up anger. He worked without rest in the hot sun till his head hurt and his skin burned black. The pain was punishment for neglecting his family, he reasoned. Losing them was the ultimate test of endurance.

At the end of the week when rations were issued, Tepu felt ashamed that he still had the same amount as when his mother and Tarema were alive. After a few weeks his feelings of guilt subsided and his sense of injustice grew.

Night was a useful tool for Tepu. He used it to plan his revenge. Hours before dawn he would walk all the way to Anbwido, dodging any patrols. He used the black stone to heighten his senses, especially his vision, and he learned how to call like a noddy, attracting the birds in night flight. Their noisy chatter was a perfect diversion when patrols loomed too close.

Filled with hatred, Tepu spied on the Japanese. His focus was Egirow. Determined to find where he went and what he did, most nights Tepu spied on the Japs from the safety of the forest. As dawn stretched into the sky he would flee back to the border of Baringa and Yamek where the work gangs assembled.

Tepu's nightly research was lonely but rewarding. One morning as he was about to emerge from his hiding place amongst the pinnacles he was startled by footsteps approaching down the Witch Track.

He sunk to the ground and watched at ankle height: Egirow hurried uphill with black boots and sword flashing, then slunk into the scrub to his left.

Tepu waited, then followed at a safe distance. A smaller overgrown track led him to a clearing peppered with dry beach almond leaves and stunted ferns. Uphill to the right was a stand of pinnacles at least ten feet high. Tepu crouched in the cover of the undergrowth to the side of the clearing and waited.

Egirow emerged from the cluster of pinnacles, strode past Tepu's hiding place and headed back down the track.

At last, Tepu had found it—Egirow's secret place. He crept over to the pinnacles for a thorough look. Inside the cluster was a space just big enough to curl up in, and on a natural ledge lay a book and a small metal tin. Tepu smiled to himself.

At home in her room Lily pushed the bolt across on the wobbly catch, then pressed her back against the door and slid down to the cool of the lino. The movie of what happened at the beach kept replaying in her mind. What was Hector doing? He must have been following her. The stupid bastard had interrupted everything. Now she had no idea when she'd see Jonah again. There was school of course, but she didn't want to see him at school, she wanted to spend time with him alone. Dumb shit Hector. *Ngaitirre!*

She looked around her room and saw the mattress had tipped to one side, twisting in the middle, but not quite falling to the floor. Lily knew something wasn't right. She always leant her mattress up so that it never tipped. Someone had been in her room last night, when she'd slept at the bunker. What had the arseholes done? Tried to steal my things? She crawled over to the clothes chest and saw the hilt of the sword poking out from behind it. She sighed with relief, but what about her blue box of hands?

She opened the chest and found the little blue box sitting just where she'd left it. She picked out her favourite item, the piece of coral. How could it be like that, she wondered, so perfect, when my own hand is so weird? Or perhaps the coral was deformed too? It had even twisted into a type of thumb, where one of the tendrils had grown lower and slanted inwards, opposite the others.

Perhaps that's what God does, she thought, picks us

up in our sleep and turns us over in his hands. Maybe he looks at me and says, 'hmm, pretty half dead for a human, but I guess she looks like a good piece of coral.'

She smiled at her fantasy and put the coral back in the box. She placed it on the floor and pulled the mattress down beside it. Then she took out a bed sheet from the wooden chest and turned off the light. She lay on the mattress with the sheet wrapped around her, reliving the scene at the beach. She was furious that Jonah had walked away, but knew he had no choice. That arsehole Hector, she'd murder him if she got the chance.

A tapping at the louvres woke her and the whisper of her name made her heart freeze for just a moment.

'Lily, wake up,' came Jonah's voice from outside.

She sat up, her pulse pounding in her throat.

'What are you doing here?' she whispered as she pulled herself up to the window and peered into the night air.

'Come out, Lil. Come with me down to the beach.'

'How did you get here?'

'From the hotel...my cousins were drinking there. They think I'm still asleep in the back of the Landrover.'

She could smell his sweet breath. 'You're drunk, aren't you?'

'Come on out, Lil,' he said impatiently.

'Shut up,' she hissed, 'you'll wake everyone up.'

'Lil, they won't know, come out, come down to the beach.'

She took a deep breath. Should she risk it? What did it mean that Jonah was drunk? Still, it was her chance now, and she knew he must really like her if he was brave enough to come to her window at night. 'OK, wait, I'll meet you down there.'

She fumbled about for her thongs in the dark and when she looked up again Jonah had gone. She eased the bolt across, cringing at the small clack it made.

The door creaked open and Lily padded through the lounge room to the back door.

twenty-four

Anbwido Leper Colony
21 May 1943

In the evening Tepu reached the outskirts of the leper colony. He hadn't ventured this close since the deaths of Tarema and his mother over a month ago. Movement at the side of a wooden hut alerted him to danger. He fell back into the shadows of the pinnacles and beach creeper. He saw a shape he knew well. It was Edouwe, carrying a bucket from one hut to another.

He made a hissing noise to attract her attention.

She stopped, looked around, then placed the bucket gently on the ground.

He hissed once more and called her name.

Checking that no one was about, she dashed to the edge of the forest to greet him.

'You're very bold,' she said, her eyes sparkling. She reached out and clasped his hands.

'Are you well?' Tepu smiled.

'We go hungry, Tepu. Sometimes we catch a few fish,

'but there is barely enough food.'

'Eat what you can,' he encouraged her. 'Even the rats have meat on them.'

'Tepu, I thought…I'd heard…they'd beaten Tarema to death.'

'Yes,' his voice trembled, 'it was my brother.'

Edouwe leant closer. 'They will catch you and kill you too if they see you here.'

'Don't fear, they won't find me,' he said. 'Meet me again, next week.'

She smiled at him, squeezed his hands, and nodded her head to the right, 'Yes, when the moon is up, in those pinnacles towards the beach.'

'I'll be there,' he whispered.

Anbwido
Friday 2 July 2004

Lorelei tossed in her sleep, lingering on the edge of wakefulness. Someone was talking in the night. 'Lily'. At the word 'Lily' she was awake in an instant. She listened into the darkness and heard snoring from the boys' room; the murmuring came from somewhere outside near Lily's room.

Trut! That girl was going to get a hiding tonight if she was caught with a boy. Trying not to make a sound, Lorelei heaved herself off the mattress. Her knees cracked as she stood and she swayed for a moment, expecting to hear the night visitor run off, but the murmuring continued.

She tiptoed down the hallway past the snoring boys and into the kitchen. The voices were clearer now.

Lorelei held her breath. She heard the bolt on Lily's door slide open. The door creaked and she knew Lily had entered the room. She waited until she could hear her unlocking the back door, then she flicked on the light.

'Going where, you *trut*?' Lorelei screamed and flew at Lily before she had a chance to open the door.

Lily blinked, stunned by the ambush and the bright light. 'The shower block...I...I need to use the toilet.'

Lorelei wrenched at her daughter's hair, pulling her head sideways and smashing it into the kitchen bench. 'You lie! I heard you talking with some boy...'

Lily clamped onto Lorelei's wrists and dug her fingernails into the sinews. Her mother swore and released her grip on Lily's hair. The girl spun free and retreated to the lounge room. 'Leave me alone, you witch!'

'You're not going outside!' Lorelei screamed and she leant heavily on the door.

'I'll do what I want!'

'What's going on?' came a groggy voice from behind Lily. Rongo stood rubbing his eyes, wearing only a *lava lava* around his waist and a pained expression. Eldon staggered behind him blinking stupidly.

'A boy, there's a boy outside!' Lorelei shrieked.

Rongo's eyes widened and he sprang at the door, pushing his mother aside, 'I'll get the bastard!'

'No!' Lily screamed, trying to follow Rongo. But Lorelei pulled her back by the arm, flinging her towards Eldon. Then she pushed the door shut and leant against it again.

Lily ran from her uncle and scrambled to her room, slamming the door behind her.

Lorelei lumbered over to the door. She pounded her fist against it. 'Come out, come out, you *trut!*' she bellowed.

She recognised the scrape of shifting furniture. Lily was barricading herself in. She'd have to break the door down now. She thudded her shoulder against it. The door bowed and flexed against her weight but it didn't break.

'Get this door open now!' she screamed at Eldon.

He hesitated, then moved to help his sister. Together they rammed their shoulders into the door and this time something cracked. The door fell open a few inches then jammed against the barricade.

'Push it, you fool, push it away from the door,' Lorelei yelled.

Eldon reached inside to push the wooden chest away. Something clanked and whooshed, then Eldon sprang back.

'Fucken! Eeiyee!'

He pulled his arm out from the doorjamb. A spray of blood painted the wall beside him.

Lorelei roared and pushed harder against the door. 'Open the door, you bitch!'

'My hand, my hand!' Eldon groaned, bumping Lorelei sideways. 'Look at my hand...' and he held up what she thought was a bloody fist. 'My fingers...'

Lorelei took a few seconds to notice in the stream of blood that there were only two fingers left on his hand.

'My fingers...' he said pressing his hand to his chest.

He backed away from her in shock, his mouth open and a spreading stain darkening the front of his T-shirt.

'Jesus!' Lorelei screamed. 'Your shirt. Wrap it in your shirt.' She lunged after him. In her efforts to help her brother, she didn't see Lily emerge with the sword and slip out the back door.

twenty-five

Anbwido Leper Colony
30 June 1943

'They've sent my parents away, and my sisters, even baby Rita,' Edouwe whispered.

'What do you mean?' Tepu asked. He held her hand and they sat together in the darkness, enclosed by pinnacles and beach creeper, on the edge of Baringa Bay.

'Last night, in a big ship, they took my cousins away too. But not just mine, everyone who has relatives at the leper colony went in a big ship. Only a few of us…carers who stay at the colony, like me…well they didn't take us.'

'Where did they send them?'

'I don't know, no one knows. Maybe they'll blow them up, or take them back to Japan and eat them.' She leant against him for comfort and he hugged her tightly to him. Her hair smelt of coconut oil and it was soft and greasy against his cheek.

'Why have those evil men come here? How much longer will they stay?' she said. 'I hate them.'

'They will die soon, Edouwe. They will die for all they've done and then we must marry.'

'Marry!' she said snuggling closer. 'Yes, we will marry.'

Tepu grinned. He'd asked her in such an off-hand way and it worked. There was no romance, no glamour. But she'd accepted him. He wanted to leap to his feet and shout with happiness, but they had to stay hidden. Instead he smiled at his fortune, praying that the war would end soon.

Anbwido
Friday 2 July 2004

Hector hid his bike in the long grass beside the pillbox near Lily's house. In the blackness he felt his way up onto its surface. It was still warm from the day's heat. The warmth was welcoming as the wind off the sea made him shiver in the night air.

What he really wanted to do was go to Lil's house and tell her what he'd found, but she was too angry to talk to him. Never mind, it was a small island and there would be a right time. She'd talk to him soon enough when she realised that Jonah was just a dumb shit like the rest of them.

Hector had crept out after his *ibu* had fallen asleep. He wanted to tell Ibu about the skull, but he thought Lil should be the first to know. And Ibu would want to take control and tell them what to do. Right now he didn't want advice, he just wanted to talk to Lily.

He lay watching the stars, wondering whether the

ghost would come to him or not and somewhere in his thoughts he fell asleep.

When he woke the warmth had almost gone from the pillbox. His bones were sore, as if someone had stretched him like a plastic dolly then let his arms and legs spring back to off-centre. He sat up and rolled his head from side to side to relieve the stiffness in his neck.

A movement to his left startled him and he flattened himself against the pillbox, turning his head slowly to make out what it was.

A figure staggered along the beach. He couldn't be sure but he thought from the way he moved it might be Jonah. He looked drunk. What was he doing here? Creeping around Lily's house, I'll bet. Bastard! Hector spat his envy out into the sand. There was nothing he could do. He couldn't stop them this time. He couldn't risk hanging around any girl's house at night. Shit, Jonah was such an arsehole. What was he thinking? He'd get himself killed if they caught him.

Certain now it was Jonah, he watched him move past the bunker and continue up the beach until the darkness ate him. Hector dropped down onto the sand. He breathed deeply and scratched his head. Should he follow or just wait here? No, he had to go. He had to see what Jonah would do. He crept up the beach at a safe distance and listened into the night.

Soon enough he heard a faint tapping sound. He edged along the path until he saw the house in the distance. Jonah's figure was lost in the shadows against the wall. Hector heard him speaking but he dared not move any closer. He stood on the path as motionless as a pinnacle, controlling his breathing and hoping that Lily wouldn't wake up.

Suddenly a light flared in the house and Jonah ran from the shadows, bolting towards him. Hector fled to the beach, making for the safety of the pillbox again. He heard shouts from the house, a door slam and panting from Jonah running behind him. Hope they catch him, the arsehole, he thought as he reached the side of the pillbox and crawled in.

The pillbox stank of urine, dead fish and stale beer. He perched on the rubble wondering what other rubbish was inside with him.

He saw Jonah's silhouette approaching and heard someone shout from behind. Jonah turned, looked back, tripped, then got to his feet again, making straight for the pillbox.

Hector froze and braced himself for another occupant, but Jonah pulled himself up onto the roof of the pillbox and was gone from sight.

'*Ngaitirre!*' Jonah cried out, then gasped in pain. Hector hoped he'd hurt himself badly.

'What the...stupid shit bicycle,' he heard Jonah exclaim, then he heard nothing more. Hector grinned, imagining how Jonah would have jumped off the pillbox and landed on his bike. Then he thought again and cursed silently: Jonah had probably ridden off on it.

He was about to emerge when another figure loomed into view. Puffing and swearing, Rongo reached the pillbox and lugged himself onto the dome.

'Bastard!' he bellowed into the night. 'The police will get you, you arsehole. You wait!'

Hector didn't move. He held his breath until he thought his brain had begun to spin. He heard Rongo land heavily in the grass on the other side of the pillbox and at last he let himself breathe out. He waited a moment or two then crawled outside. He pulled himself up onto the dome and looked out to the roadside. A pale shape in the distance walked along the side of the road back towards Lily's house; it was Rongo in his *lava lava*.

Hector waited until Rongo disappeared then he jumped down into the grass and felt around in the shadows for his bike. Just as he'd feared, it was gone. Jonah was probably half way to Pago on it by now, the bastard! Hector would have to steal himself another one.

He sighed. The day had been so stuffed up and now his bike had gone. Shit! What was the point of it all? He climbed back onto the pillbox and stared out into the blackness of the sea.

'Hector, is that you?' came Lily's voice from the beach.

'Yeah,' he said warily. Was she about to tell him to piss off again? Then he saw her emerge, her shoulders slumped. She dragged the sword behind her in the sand.

'What are you doing?' he said. 'Are you OK?'

'I need help,' she said.

twenty-six

Anbwido
July 1943

Each night Tepu ventured out to call the ancestor bird. Now he knew Egirow's secret place he could execute his plan. He would surprise Egirow one morning. But Tepu was weak from hunger and Egirow was armed. How could he overpower the marine? It would involve the black stone, the only magic he had. He trusted that the bird would show him how to use the stone to defeat Egirow.

Once he'd communed with his ancestor he walked south, skirting patrols, to spend the nights in Anbwido.

Sometimes he met Edouwe near the leper colony. If the bombers came they huddled in the pinnacles. He covered her as each blast shook the ground but they dared not leave their hiding place for fear of being caught. She never stayed with him long, however, because her grandparents would be alarmed by her absence. Once the raid was over she ran off, hidden by the night to slip back to the leper colony.

Tepu then walked through the forest and slept beside the Witch Track. He knew he had to watch Egirow's movements to know precisely when the Lieutenant would come to his secret place. Usually it was early morning, pre-dawn. The sound of his quick footsteps roused Tepu from his dreams.

The Lieutenant spent half an hour or more in his secret place. Tepu listened each time. Egirow would mutter a litany and then there was silence. Was it some kind of spiritual ritual? Tepu could only guess, but it struck him that Egirow was calling on his own Japanese ancestor gods.

They have no power here, Tepu thought. My magic will defeat them.

During the day Tepu laboured with a strength that astonished the other men. He had only two thoughts: what it felt like to be with Edouwe and what it *would* feel like to kill Egirow. Both thoughts burned into his mind and drove him to go on regardless of the heat, the pain and the gnawing hunger.

Anbwido
Friday 2 July 2004

Lily was trapped like a little fish in a rock pool. There was nowhere to go and nothing to stop them coming in after her. She'd pushed the bolt across but knew it wouldn't hold. She felt the door bow when they pushed on it. Even the barricade she'd set up wouldn't keep Lorelei back.

She leant against the clothes chest, straining to keep it against the door.

In the dim light she saw the sword glint. She lunged across the room for it. Then came the rip of wood splitting and Lily knew the lock had broken. The clothes chest scraped across the floor. Lily dived back to strengthen the barricade and crushed something underfoot. The sword fell to the floor beside her. She fumbled about for it but felt instead her little wooden box, squashed and splintered—her box of hands. Why her box of treasures? Everything was ruined, they wrecked everything! Rage seethed inside her. Everything she loved had been smashed or spoilt by her family.

A shadow curled around the door, attempting to push the barricade away. Furious, Lily grabbed the sword off the floor and struck at it. There was a thud like a Chinaman cleaving meat and she knew she'd hit her clothes chest.

'Fucken!' Eldon roared from behind the door.

'Get away!' she screamed. She wrenched the sword free from the wood and raised it ready to strike again, expecting a second attempt, but the door was still and a kind of wailing had begun. 'My hand, my hand! Look at my hand!' she heard Eldon cry.

She climbed onto the clothes chest and peeked into the lounge room. Lorelei was fumbling with Eldon's T-shirt, pushing him backwards while he howled like an injured dog, stumbling away from her.

Lily slipped out of the house and fled down the path to the beach, still clutching the sword. I've hurt him, I've hurt the bastard. He deserves it though, the way he hurt me. She hoped she'd cut him badly too, hoped she'd chopped his hand off. Those hands that had mauled her wouldn't touch her now. He wouldn't dare. She was strong and fierce and no one would hurt her again. No one would push her around anymore. Not Eldon, not Lorelei, not anyone.

She clenched her fists but her left hand felt strangely numb and heavy, her fingers stiff. The sensation flowed up her arm, making her shudder. It's just a reaction to what happened, she reasoned, just a build up of tension.

How would Eldon and Lorelei react to her now? They probably wouldn't let her back in the house. That would be fine. She never wanted to live there again.

But where would she stay? Decima was still in Australia. There was nowhere to go. She couldn't stay at Hector's. That would be against custom and anyway, Hector had infuriated her today: followed her, spied on her, mucked up her plans.

She remembered Christina's words. 'You're welcome here, anytime…when you need to escape…' Anytime—did that mean midnight when you're running away from trouble? Not likely.

She ran along the beach in the moonlight and headed for the only sanctuary she knew: the pillbox. Those fat arseholes couldn't fit in, so she knew she would be safe. And she had the sword with her; no one was going to scare her anymore. The pillbox would do for now. In the daylight she'd make her way up to Christina's house.

And Jonah; where was he now? Drunk and running

away into the night somewhere. He hadn't stuck around. He wasn't here for her now. He wasn't any different from all the others. He had wanted her to follow him to Leper Beach. What would have happened if Hector hadn't interrupted? Would he have forced her just like Eldon? Maybe he really was like Eldon and she just couldn't see it. No, he wasn't like the others. But then he *was* drunk, drunk and stupid, wanting her to go down to the beach. To do what? Just kiss, or something more? Stupid shit, why did he have to get drunk?

She saw someone climb onto the pillbox in front of her; for an instant she thought it was Jonah and her doubts about him faded. He had come back for her. Then she recognised the shape; it was Hector.

Something inside her was relieved to see him. The knot of resentment vanished. Hector wouldn't desert her. She knew he would help. She called out to him.

'Are you sure this is the best thing to do?' Lily whispered to Hector.

Together they peered over the terrace wall. The security light wasn't on. The house was completely blacked out. Lily could barely make out the wash house on the far side of the terrace.

'No Tevuans will look for it here, and if Christina or her dad find it, they can take it back to Australia with them. No more ghosts, no more problems. Anyway, you're the one who doesn't want to let go of it. At least it's safe here.' He sprang onto the wall and helped Lily over.

'Let go, I can manage myself,' she growled, pushing him away.

'Quick then!' he urged as he crept over to the wash house.

Lily ran along the terrace as lightly as she could, but her thongs click clacked on the pavings. She followed Hector through the door and pushed it shut. It was so dark inside that she fumbled about like a blind person, prodding Hector in the back.

'*Suh!* Watch it.'

'I can't see!'

He grabbed her free hand and guided it towards the bench. 'Here, put the sword under here so it sits on the pipes. They won't see it.'

'I don't want to leave it.'

'You have to! Don't you understand, it's a weapon. If he's hurt bad then the police will want it. You can't keep it.'

He didn't add that she might have killed Eldon with it. He'd said that earlier, when he tried to convince her to throw it into the sea. She'd washed the blood off but she couldn't part with it. She couldn't even bear to let go of it. Hector then said they should take it to Riki, but she knew Lorelei would look for her there. Christina's wash house was the compromise. She'd leave the sword here and they'd go and wake up Riki and ask his advice.

That was the plan but Lily sensed that it wouldn't work. The desire to keep the sword with her was overwhelming. Her stained hand clenched the hilt so tightly that all sensation had drained from her fist. Her arm was numb with cold, a ghostly cold that chilled her veins.

She bent down to put the sword under the bench but a sudden noise and burst of light startled her. She turned to see the glare of a flashlight.

'What the hell's going on?' said Christina.

twenty-seven

Anbwido
5 July 1943

Tepu heard the marines approaching. He sank low, his face inches from the forest floor. He expected to see a band of men marching, but what he saw shocked him. They had a girl with them. It was Edouwe.

They pulled her along by her hair like a horse. Her hands were bound and one of the marines had a bayonet at her back. Her face was spattered with mud and one of her knees was grazed; a trickle of blood outlined her shin. What had they done to her?

Tepu saw the leer in the marines' eyes. He knew what they intended. Tepu's chest tightened with horror. His girl would be spoilt before his eyes. He had to stop their attack, but they would beat or kill him if he tried. He forced himself not to move, though every muscle in his body was ready.

Government Settlement
Anbwido
Saturday 3 July 2004

Christina couldn't sleep. The power had gone off for the third time during her stay and the overhead fan that normally clunked away was silent. The heat was so oppressive that she imagined being in a toaster. An overpowering smell of mould grew in the still air. Sweat pooled beneath her, the bed sheets clung to her skin. She turned from side to side in an effort to get comfortable but it was no use. Hot and irritable, she lurched out of bed to get a drink of water.

She crept past her father's room, feeling her way down the hall to the kitchen. He wouldn't wake up no matter how hot it was. He was used to the tropical climate, and he'd drunk a few too many beers after dinner. They'd sat up and talked but the conversation turned to her mother and his tone grew bitter. Christina had gone to bed and left him to his drinking.

Now it was after midnight and the moon cast a pale light on the terrace outside the kitchen window. Christina saw two figures scampering over to the laundry. She blinked hard. Was she dreaming? She couldn't be certain but the second silhouette, a female, was thickset and ran just like Lily. But if it was Lily, what was she doing here, at this time of night? Unless there'd been trouble. Christina grabbed the torch off the top of the fridge and sneaked outside.

She tiptoed across the terrace. She heard whispering inside the wash house. What if it were two people she didn't know at all? She took a deep breath, pushed the door open and switched on the torch. Hector and Lily were crouched on the ground. It looked as if they were tampering with the plumbing.

'What the hell's going on?'

'*Ngaitirre!* Put that torch away,' Hector hissed.

'No, I won't! What are you doing?'

Lily and Hector exchanged worried glances before Hector finally said: 'We're hiding something.'

Christina saw the pain on Lily's face and wondered if her friend was about to burst into tears. She clutched the same sword she had on the day they first met. There were small dark spots on her T-shirt. It looked like blood. 'You can tell me...I can help,' Christina said.

Lily hurriedly related the night's events. Hector interjected about his stolen bike and how Lily's brother had sworn to ring the police. Now they both assumed that Rongo had mistaken the fleeing boy for Hector.

'I think you need to tell the police the truth and give them the sword,' Christina said.

They both looked at her as if she'd turned into an octopus. 'I can't go to the police, they've been after me for months,' Hector said.

'And I can't let go of the sword,' Lily said flatly. 'It's stuck to my hand.'

Christina didn't believe her. 'It's probably just shock,' she said. 'Let me look.' She clasped Lily's arm and was surprised at how icy it felt. The cold seemed to spread to her own fingertips. 'Eerr!' she said, pulling back in fright.

'See, it's bewitched,' Lily said. 'It's making my hand die.'

'Riki would know what to do,' Hector said.

'But if the police go to the hut, they'll catch us.'

Christina calculated the odds: Lily's family would only contact the police after they'd taken Eldon to the hospital, if at all. Eldon would probably be too ashamed to get the police involved. 'We should go to Riki straight away and if the police are hanging around I can distract them,' she said.

'You...you don't have to help,' Lily said.

Christina recalled the first time she'd helped them avoid the police. She was frightened of Lily then. When Decima told her about Lily's home life she felt sorry for Lily. Fear and pity weren't the most honourable reasons to help somebody, but now she wanted to help because they were friends. It was probably unwise to get caught up but she could at least help them get to the hut.

'Come on,' she said, 'before my torch batteries run out.'

They made their way along the Witch Track in silence. When they reached the turn-off that led to the hut Hector told Christina to switch off the torch.

'I think there's a car outside,' he whispered.

They staggered along in the dark, clinging to one another, edging closer to the hut.

'I can hear voices,' Lily whispered.

They slipped behind a tomano tree and peered into the blackness. There were no lights on anywhere. The black-out must have affected all of Anbwido, Christina thought. Over on the porch she heard the old man cough. She could hear people speaking in Tevuan. One of them moved away and opened a car door. Moments later the engine revved and headlights flashed, lighting up the forest where they were hiding.

twenty-eight

Edouwe cried out and one of the marines slapped her.

'Listen to the thief cry,' one said.

'She'll cry some more now,' said another, slapping her too. Then he forced her to the ground.

Edouwe struggled wildly but she couldn't fight off four men.

Two marines held her arms, pinning them to the ground while the one who had pushed her fought to keep her thrashing legs still.

Tepu had to help her, but he dared not move. If they found him during curfew hours he would be punished, but he couldn't bear the torture before him.

In a burst of fury he sprang out from the bushes just as Egirow shouted at his men from the other direction.

Hector wrenched Christina sideways, pulling her to the ground beside him. Lily pressed herself against the tree. She held her breath, hoping they hadn't been seen.

The engine rumbled, then the car moved towards them, the glare of the headlights intensifying.

'What do we do now?' Christina whimpered.

'Wait,' Hector said, 'they're just turning around.'

Lily heard the gears crunch. The headlights swung away. Hector was right. The car drove down the hill towards the Ring Road.

Once it had gone they scurried over to the hut. A kerosene lamp glowed in the kitchen. Riki was lighting a small gas cooker when the three of them filed in through the door. He turned to them and shook his head. 'What have you done, Hector?' he murmured. 'The police were here looking for you.'

'What did you tell them?'

'Nothing. I never tell police anything,' he said.

'Will they come back?' Christina asked.

Riki laughed. 'They hate coming here, they won't come back. They don't want to work, they just play cards or sleep.' He rubbed his brown belly and tightened his *lava lava*. 'Now why are you here late? What did you do?' he said softly.

'It's the sword,' Lily mumbled, holding it out towards him. 'It's made my hand dead.'

Riki limped forward, his bowed legs creaking. He reached out, caressed the blade and, lifting it close to his face, sniffed deeply. 'It cuts again,' he pronounced under his breath.

'What do you mean?'

'There is fresh blood.'

Lily cringed and turned to Hector for support, but he looked away as if he knew nothing.

They'd washed it together in the sea. They were sure it was clean. How did the old man know? She looked at Riki and shook her head.

The old man stared at her. 'What did you do?' he whispered.

She shivered. Although she didn't want to look at him, she felt her eyes being drawn to his. She was certain he could read her soul.

'An accident,' she muttered. She could feel herself shaking and her lip quivered as though tears would come, but she fought them back, determined not to cry in front of Hector or the old man. 'He tried to get in my room... I hate him.'

A long silence filled the kitchen until the old man said, 'I hated once too, hated enough to hurt a man.'

'Who?' Hector asked.

Riki ignored him. 'The man, he is alive—or you kill him?'

She took a deep breath. Her chest grew tight until the pressure was too much and the words raced out of her mouth, 'He's OK, I think.'

'Good,' the old man said. He leant back against the wall and nodded as if he knew the whole story even though she'd said so little.

'We've got to get rid of the sword. The police will look for it,' Christina said.

'The police?' Riki smiled and began to chuckle. 'I don't think so. We must take the sword to the real owner. He'll tell us what to do.'

'Do you mean the ghost?' Hector said.

'Mmm.' The old man raised his eyebrows and gazed at them with a peaceful expression, but Lily noticed that he held his breath. It was almost a minute before he spoke again. 'Where did you find the sword?'

'Up in the bush here, just off the Witch Track,' Lily pointed.

The old man stiffened and shut his eyes.

'But Ibu, that's not all,' Hector's words tumbled out. 'I found a body there too.'

Christina gasped.

Lily was stunned. Why hadn't Hector told her? She glared at him, willing him to explain, but Riki had begun to tremble. He sat with his eyes closed. It looked as if his eyelids were stretched thin and his long rubbery face frightened her. When he stopped shaking he spoke, his voice a whisper. 'Tell me more,' he said.

'It's just bones—a skull and things. It must be him, Ibu. The skull is only a few metres from where we found the sword.'

Riki closed his eyes. 'It must be our ghost. Tell me, Lily, what does he look like?'

Lily sighed and shut he eyes. 'He's got a baseball cap with an anchor on it...he's got long black boots... he shouts at me all the time but I can't hear him...

he looks like a Chinaman.'

'Where did you see him? What did he do?' Riki asked. The shadows from the lamp made his eyes seem hollow and his nose loomed bigger than ever.

'At my house and at the pillbox. He held up his arm like this,' she said, mimicking the raised fist.

'It is a marine,' Riki said. 'He wants to raise his sword but it's lost.' He coughed. 'What does he say?'

'He never says anything,' Lily said.

Riki nodded, 'It is good. It must be the same one.' He sat quietly for a long time, scratching the stubble on his chin. Finally he said, 'We must put him to rest.' He reached up to the shelves above the sink and took down the bottle Hector had found. 'He will speak this time.' He nodded at Hector. 'You show me. We'll go now and give him the sword.'

'How?' Lily whined. 'I can't let go, I can't get rid of it.'

'It is his spirit. It's poisoning you, Lily. We must give it back.'

'No,' Lily heard herself say. 'I don't want to.'

'But it's evil, it's a bad thing, this sword,' Riki said softly.

'No, I need it.' Her words echoed about the room.

The old man looked at her squarely. 'You don't need it anymore. Before it gave courage to you, now all it gives you is pain and death. I know what they do. They are evil these swords. The marines killed many islanders. Chop, chop. They cut the necks of every one. Good people died because the marines were cruel. Already this sword has made you cruel.'

She looked down at the floor.

Riki laid his hand on her shoulder. 'Many people are cruel and hurt others,' he said. 'We must not be afraid of the memories—even when they hurt so much. The stories are important—they teach us something.' Then he turned to Hector. 'Get some torches. I'll get a bucket. Our marine must rest tonight.'

twenty-nine

Anbwido
5 July 1943

'Leper!' Tepu screamed at them.

They all turned at once and faced him with blank faces.

'Leper, she's a leper!' he yelled, gesturing at his fingers and toes. They didn't understand and the nearest marine moved forward to grab him.

But now Egirow was snapping at them in their own language. '*Rai-byo no onna,*' he barked and instantly they recoiled from Edouwe.

The marines shouted, howled and cursed each other. They wiped their hands on the nearest leaves in a furious dance of disgust and shame.

In that moment of confusion Edouwe vanished into the forest. Tepu turned to run too, but Egirow caught him round the head with his rifle butt. Tepu spun and fell to the ground. He struggled to regain his footing but Egirow was quicker, kicking the wind out of his lungs. Tepu gasped for air. The last thing he remembered that morning was the thrust of Egirow's boot in his face.

The Witch Track
Anbwido
Saturday 3 July 2004

Hector led the way along the Witch Track. Even though he had company he felt his breath rattle with every step. He swung the torch about so the beam wouldn't reveal his shaking hand.

'It's up here,' he said, his voice fast and squeaky. Coughing to clear his throat, he pushed past overgrown bushes. The clearing opened before them and Hector pointed the torch beam up the hill to his right, illuminating a stand of thin trees.

'This is where we found the sword. The bones are in there…behind the trees,' he said.

Riki hung his head and muttered something into his chest.

'I wonder how he died?' Lily said.

No one answered her. Hector fought off an urge to run home, but he couldn't run because he had to show how brave he was. Lily and Christina inched closer to him. He sensed their trembling. But the old man was not afraid. He stepped towards the trees, put down his bucket and beckoned for the light to come closer.

Hector hesitated. The air about him chilled. He didn't want to disturb any evil ghosts but he wanted to see what would happen.

'Bring the sword, girl,' the old man called.

Lily twitched and clutched at Hector's T-shirt. Her eyes were staring. 'My arm's so cold,' she croaked.

'It's OK, Ibu will fix it,' Hector whispered, although he had no idea how, and when he looked towards the trees his *ibu* had vanished.

'Shit, where's he gone?' Christina said, switching on her torch and scanning the forest.

'I don't know,' said Hector. Had his *ibu* deserted them? He struggled to control his thoughts. Of course he wouldn't do such a thing, but Hector felt abandoned. He couldn't bear looking at the trees where the skull lay, so he shone the torch at his feet instead. The three of them huddled together, the sword still gripped in Lily's left hand. They were a tight knot in a small pool of light.

Then Hector heard Riki cough somewhere nearby. Leaves rustled and branches snapped. The old man hobbled back into the clearing. Hector and Christina swung their torch beams on him.

He looked enormous illuminated by both lights. He held two leafy branches and chewed something crunchy. Saliva dripped from his mouth. He dropped the branches at the base of the trees, then came over to Lily. He spat into his free hand. 'Be still,' he said, wiping the mush from his mouth down the length of her frozen arm. As he did so he chanted some strange words. Then he massaged her limb so roughly that Hector thought she would cry out, but Lily stood motionless.

'Give me the sword,' he commanded.

Lily raised her hand, flexing her fingers. Moving with

mechanical stiffness they slowly released their grip on the sword.

Riki took it from her and placed it at the foot of the trees. Taking up the discarded branches he stood motionless for an instant then breathed deeply. Each exhalation was a loud rushing puff. He raised the branches above his head and shook them, chanting in a language Hector didn't recognise.

The old man shuddered and puffed as he sang, bringing down the branches in sharp brushing motions about the sword and the tree trunks, as if he were swatting at flies. Then suddenly his shoulders slumped and he placed the branches beside the sword. He turned to face Hector, Lily and Christina.

'We are safe now,' he said, 'the anger is gone from this place. Bring the light close, boy, you must help me.'

Hector couldn't move. He'd never seen his *ibu* dance and chant like that. Was his *ibu* a witch? Was it true what everyone said, that his *ibu* was crazy? His head was spinning.

It was Christina who nudged him forward. His feet jerked to life and carried him over to his grandfather who knelt at the base of the trees. Even though the anger had gone from this place, an unbearable cold remained that made him shake.

'I...I think I can feel the air now, Ibu,' he said.

'Yes, he is here—yes, I see him,' the old man said as he reached in through the trees. His big fingers shovelled under the skull and eased it from the ground. 'Bring the bucket,' he said.

Hector retrieved the bucket, pulled out the bottle and placed them both beside the old man. He stood to move away but his *ibu* caught him by the arm.

'Go in now, boy, go through the trees and dig around for more bones.'

Hector froze. Not inside where the body lay—he didn't want to do it.

'Go now, you're a small size.'

'It's OK,' Christina said behind him, 'Lily and I will shine the torches.' One of the girls squeezed his shoulder, encouraging him.

Hector took a deep breath then pushed through the screen of branches and knelt in the earth. It was damp and gritty against his legs. After five minutes and a lot of digging and prodding he found more bones, smaller ones, pieces of spine and ribs and arms. They were cold in his hands. He passed them out to his *ibu* who placed them all in the bucket.

'No more. I think that's all there is.'

'It's not very many,' Christina said.

'I think rats and crabs, and rain and wild pigs have been before us. That's all there is,' said Riki.

'I want to come out now,' Hector said.

'No,' Riki said, passing a torch through to him, 'go into the pinnacles, bring back these things: the tin and the black stone.'

Hector stared at his grandfather and shook his head. 'We've got the bones, let's go!'

'It's not finished yet, Hector...do as I say,' Riki urged.

Reluctantly Hector took the torch and crawled

forward. There were pinnacles on either side of him and one far in front, which formed a small room of rock. He stood up and shone the torch around. The pinnacle directly opposite had a shelf carved into its surface. On it lay a metal tin covered with a smooth black stone. A tin and a stone—how did Ibu know? He picked them up and put them in his pocket. The stone was heavy and warm against his thigh.

Hector crawled out from the bushes, pulled the objects from his pocket and gave them to his grandfather. Ibu sighed as he took the stone and let it roll across his palm before he gave it a squeeze. Then he handed it back to Hector. 'You will need this magic now. Keep it safe,' he said.

Hector wondered what he meant about magic. He watched his *ibu* place the tin beside the sword and the bucket of bones. Then the old man picked up the bottle and took a few steps back. 'Off the light,' he said.

Hector and Lily turned off the torches. The black of the forest surrounded them. 'Shit!' Hector jumped as Lily's hand pawed at his shoulder. Christina stifled a nervous laugh.

'Quiet!' the old man barked. 'Be still, he must talk.'

They stood in silence, waiting for something to happen. Lily clutched Hector's arm and her breath warmed his ear. Apart from her closeness and the heat of the stone in his pocket, Hector felt chilled to his bones. If it weren't for his heart thumping in his chest he might have been snap cooled like a fish in a freezer. As Hector's eyes adjusted to the night he heard a soft droning, a humming that must have been Ibu blowing over the neck of the bottle.

Then a drifting haze of light formed above the place where the sword was lying. Hector gasped as he felt Lily's fingernails dig into his arm. Behind them Christina swore softly and huddled closer. The figure of a man stood in front of them, faded and yellowy-green. He wore a small peaked cap, sandy uniform and high black boots, and he rested his hand on a long sword at his side. The handle was decorated with a row of diamond shapes. Slowly he raised the sword in front of his face and held it steady.

Hector wanted to run, but his feet were leaden. Except for the warmth against his thigh the cold seemed to claw about him; even the girls' radiant heat had leached away.

'Where will you lie, *yani egirow*?' Riki asked.

Hector heard the word 'Baringa' howl about him but it was unlike any spoken voice he knew and the shrill tone lingered like the ringing of a bell.

'Be at peace,' Ibu said and at once the image bowed forward and disappeared.

Hector tried to lift his trembling legs. 'Can I shine the torch now?' he said, but his voice came out as a squeak.

'Yes, we go now,' Riki said, 'we go to Baringa to say goodbye.'

thirty

Tepu had been selected to join a group of men for a task on the outskirts of Anbwido. It had surprised him, since he didn't feel fit. He'd taken five days to recover from Egirow's beating the week before.

Now the marines ordered them to round up all the people at the leper colony and help carry their possessions to the reef. There would be a boat perhaps, like the ship that took their relatives away. If only Tepu could go with them, be with Edouwe and escape this torture together.

He saw her walking in the middle of the group, holding two woven mats and a basket, no doubt the only belongings she and her grandparents had. She smiled when she saw him and found her way over to the edge of the group. She walked just in front of him with her head down.

'Where are they taking us? I don't want to leave you,' she said, talking to her feet.

'I don't know what's going on. Be brave,' he whispered.

The marines shouted at them to move faster and keep quiet. So they walked in silence to Baringa Bay and Tepu was filled with dread.

Baringa Bay Channel
Saturday 3 July 2004

Lorelei drove home from the hospital where she'd left Eldon and Rongo. The moonlight shone over Baringa Bay making it look like a professional photograph. She yawned, then peered into the distance. There was someone at the channel. She had seen the pale yellow light, but now there was nothing. Stupid arseholes, what were people doing on the reef before dawn? Must be keen fishermen, she thought. She slowed the Landrover, cut the lights and engine and rolled to a stop in the grey predawn light. Out on the reef four figures waded a few metres out, carrying what looked like fishing tackle. But wait—she knew that walk, that silhouette—one of them was Lily.

Lorelei rolled out of the vehicle and stomped to the channel's edge. 'Where do you think you're going?' she bellowed.

The figures paused and turned; the one that was Lily almost ran but the bigger one grabbed her, spoke to her, then pushed her forward. She walked back through the shallows dragging something along behind her.

'You're in trouble girl, better come home now,' Lorelei called.

Lily marched slowly up the channel ramp and stopped a few metres short of her mother. 'I'm not going home. I'm not going anywhere with you,' she said.

Lorelei felt a familiar rage build inside her. She strode towards her, 'Come home now!' she ordered.

'You deaf? I said I'm not coming home. I've got something I have to do.' She lifted the sword up in front of her eyes and held it still.

Lorelei stopped, transfixed by the sword. So this was Lily's weapon. She looked from Lily to the others on the reef. Had the weird old Gilbert man made her daughter crazy too?

'Come on, girl. Don't you go around with crazy people,' she whispered, edging closer.

'They're good people, they're my friends.'

'Lily, the old man's mad, you know that…'

'Don't come any closer,' Lily hissed, pointing the sword at Lorelei's neck. The metal gleamed in the half-light and Lorelei saw that it didn't shake; Lily's grip was firm.

Lorelei paused, wondering how to distract her daughter or calm her down. 'Eh, what you doing? Put it down, Lil. Don't be stupid,' she said, backing off.

'I'm not stupid. You touch me and I'll cut you.'

Lorelei struggled for the right words. How was she to convince the stupid bitch to come home? How was she going to get her to put down that sword? 'Lily, you're already in trouble, what you did to Eldon and having that boy at the house. Don't make it worse.'

'It already is worse. What you did to me, what he did to me.'

'What about what you've done to Eldon? I've just left the hospital. He's lost three fingers, you bitch,' Lorelei screamed at her.

Lily pushed forward, her eyes wild and bulging. She pressed the sword up against Lorelei's throat and leered into her mother's face.

'Good, then he won't touch me again!' she said.

The words echoed in Lorelei's head. 'What do you mean, girl?'

'I mean, what happens in that house. Don't you know?'

Lorelei opened her mouth, but nothing came out.

'No—no you don't because you're never home. You're never there to protect me. So I do it myself now—see. And no bastard uncle's going to push his way in and force me ever again.'

'What are you saying?' Lorelei asked, her voice trembling as she inched backwards. Did she mean Eldon? No, it wasn't possible. Lorelei thudded against the Landrover. One of her elbows banged against the door. She winced from the pain and looked about. There was no escape. The sword, cold against her neck, pinned her to the vehicle. She looked into her daughter's face, searching for sympathy or pity but in the pale light saw only a curled top lip—just like her own. As she realised their sameness something burst in her mind, and a knot of doubt and mistrust about her younger brother unravelled. Her confidence shrivelled. She cowered as Lily, furious and strong, loomed over her.

'Eldon?' Lorelei whispered.

'Arsehole Eldon,' Lily said, spitting the words out.

Lorelei sniffed and her eyes began to twitch. How could he, her own brother. 'No, what are you saying? Stop lying!'

Lily jerked forward, pressing the sword deeper against her mother's throat. 'I'm not lying, you stupid witch, it's true! You don't care about what happens to me, do you?'

'No!' Lorelei gasped. Her head throbbed with panic as she tried to find soothing words. 'I worry when you're out at night. It's not safe.'

'Safe! It's not safe in my own house. I'm not safe with you or Eldon,' Lily said, snarling. 'How do you think it feels, to be forced?'

Lorelei swallowed hard against the pressing blade. Memories flooded her brain: the fear, the shame, the self-loathing, the hatred and the honey-skinned baby born with a guilty smear. 'Don't tell me,' she whispered, 'I already know it. How do you think you were conceived?'

thirty-one

Baringa Bay
12 July 1943

The lepers and their carers placed all their belongings in a pile on the beach and lined up on the reef as the marines instructed. Then the marines told Tepu and the other men to line up behind them.

Egirow pointed out to sea. Just off the reef a small boat rocked in the waves. Tepu knew at once what was about to happen. The Japs would send them all away, off in a small leaky boat that had no hope of floating much longer than a few days. They would reach nowhere. They would all die of starvation or exposure, or they'd drown and be the ready meal for dozens of sharks.

So this is our end, Tepu thought. Behind him was instant death: a line of Japanese with rifles pointed and bayonets fixed. Out to sea was slow death in the ocean.

There was a lull between the crashing waves. For a moment Lily stared into her mother's eyes. Tears washed the brown pupils. Red spider webs of veins within the white were more vivid than she'd ever seen them. In those eyes she saw years of suffering, self-hatred and coldness. As the surf broke against the reef once more, Lily's sympathy vanished.

'Who was it?' she rasped.

'A white man, an Australian—like your friend,' she gestured towards the reef where Christina stood.

'That's why you don't like her...and that's why you hate me,' she whispered. Then the enormity of it hit her.

'Shit!' she screamed, shoving her mother aside. The blow knocked Lorelei over onto the road. She sprawled on the bitumen, her fat legs kicking in the air.

Lily plunged the sword into the bushes beside the Landrover. She wailed and bellowed, hacking at the greenery, sending clumps of vegetation flying. The momentum of her swings echoed the heaving of her chest. '*Ngaitirre!* Arseholes!' she screamed her anger into the dawn. Scream it, shout it, bash it, cut it—but don't cry girl, you mustn't cry girl, she told herself. But she couldn't stop the flow of tears.

Gradually her shouts became moans and the wild hacking slowed. Her shoulders ached from the spent tension. Her throat burnt. She looked around self-consciously.

Lorelei struggled to stand. She didn't seem so

threatening now with her shirt all bunched up and her hair falling untidily from her bun. She waddled to the Landrover, sniffed and wiped at her face as she pulled herself in behind the wheel, staring at her daughter. 'Come home when you're ready,' she said shakily.

Lily couldn't answer. Her throat was too dry and she didn't know the words to say. She turned to the reef where Hector, Christina and Riki waited. The sky beyond them was a soft grey and the tide was going out. She strode down the ramp towards them. She had done what the old man told her. 'Don't run away,' he'd said to her. 'Use the courage you have—not the sword. Don't let it poison you again.' Even though Lorelei's words left her feeling empty and cheated, as if some huge wedge of her life had been cut away, she now understood the brokenness of her mother. She no longer feared her.

'Quick, Lil, the sun's nearly up,' Hector called from the shallows.

She waded through the puddles on the reef and felt the warm water wash over her feet.

'You must hurry, girl. Take the sword to the edge of the reef before the sun clears the water. Then do what your heart tells you,' Riki said.

Lily didn't understand what he meant, but the old man was calm and his eyes reassured her.

'We will follow behind,' he said.

She waded deeper into the water, careful not to stumble in the cracks and rockpools of the reef. When she reckoned she was only a metre or so from the edge she stopped and braced herself against the waves as they crashed through at knee height.

Out to sea the sun emerged and cast a white glow on the waves. The glare stung her eyes and she blinked, struggling to focus. Only twenty metres out, she saw an old wooden boat materialise on the water. It rocked and lolled on the black sea, rocking and lolling her memory back.

It was the same boat—the same boat she strove to swim to and never reached. The same boat she was desperate to escape to, away from Eldon, away from herself. Her memory told her to jump into the water, but she knew she would sink. Her heart told her to run, run away from her fear. She tried to shout but her voice was only a croak. She shuddered and a chill crept over her.

Terrified, she turned to her friends. They were only a few paces behind her, but as she looked at them their features blurred. Hector and Christina became indistinct like shimmers of sunlight on sea spray, but Riki stood straighter and his age fell away.

His skin was tight and gleamed with oil. He had transformed before her eyes into a tall Gilbertese youth. As she looked at him with both fear and recognition she realised he was not alone. About a dozen ghostly ragged men formed a line along the reef cutting off her retreat back to the beach. Beyond them were pairs of Japanese marines, advancing slowly with rifles pointed in her direction, and with them stood the *yani* in his black boots with his sword raised, shouting orders.

Horrified at the scene before her, Lily screamed. She tried to run to the side but she couldn't move. Her voice was drowned out by the crash of the waves.

A cold surge ran through her and she saw a figure stumble and run, as if out from her own soul. It was her own body that ran past the islanders into the line of marines beyond.

Tack, tack! A rifle sounded and the girl was shot. She lurched and fell to the reef. Riki ran to her and so did the *yani* and the two nearest marines. They pushed Riki aside and punched him, while the *yani* pointed his sword at the girl and shouted at her.

Lily screamed at him to stop but her words were taken by the ocean roar and he didn't even notice she was there.

The girl rolled to her side and wailed, a cry that Lily knew from her waking moments, a cry she had heard at Leper Beach just a few nights before.

Then the marines, each pointing their rifles at Riki, pushed him towards the girl. He held her by the shoulders and pulled her to her feet. Her left arm, torn by a bullet, hung at her side and a patch of red stained the pale rags she wore. Together they staggered forward as the two marines and the *yani* followed.

As they came level with Lily, she sensed their fear and she was sure they were both about to die. She turned back to the sea to watch their fate and was startled at the scene before her. Dozens of ghostly figures slipped off the edge of the reef into the sea. A group of black heads bobbed up and down in the swell as they made for the leaky craft ahead of them. One had already reached the boat and was hauling himself over the side.

Riki and the girl stood at the edge of the reef. He let go of her, assured her he would go first, and would catch her when she jumped in. Just as he flexed his legs to jump, one of the marines caught him by the arm and spun him around. The *yani* shouted at him. Riki flinched and cowered from the officer. Then Riki said to the girl, 'You must go first, they say. I'll be next. I'll help you.'

Lily saw the girl's terror, felt it churn within her as she peered down into the blue-black gloom. 'It's OK, I'll be with you,' Riki said, and he helped her down into the warm water. She let go of the edge and pushed herself off into the waves. Lily saw the stain of red from her arm in the sea beside her and wondered how long it would take for the sharks to come.

Lily and the girl both turned, waiting for Riki to dive in, but instead saw the *yani* punch him and push him to the ground. 'No!' Lily screamed and this time a voice rang out but it wasn't hers—it was the girl's.

'Tepu! Tepu! Tepuariki!' Her scream became a wail once more, shrill and pleading, and her head rose and sank above the rolling sea.

Riki struggled to his feet, but the *yani* kept hitting him about the head until Lily could no longer see his features because of all the blood. Then the two marines dragged him away from the edge and the *yani* drew his gun. Bwack! The girl's wailing stopped and her head sunk from view.

Lily slumped forward as if all the energy had been thumped out of her. She turned and saw Riki grow older, heavier and more familiar, until he became Hector's *ibu* once more. His face was no longer smeared with blood; now it was covered with tears.

'You saw it all. It was you, wasn't it?' she whispered.

The old man didn't answer. He merely pointed to the spot on the reef behind them. She turned to see the boat fade from view but the *yani* remained, shouting at Lily with furious hatred.

She looked down at the sword and hesitated. 'I can't give it to him, not now I've seen what he's done.'

'It's his spirit, Lily. You can't keep it. It's evil like him.'

She paused for a moment and felt the crash of the surf try to unbalance her. 'I'll give it to the sea,' she said, 'the sea will take our rubbish away.'

'Yes, the sea cleans us all.'

Lily nodded. She heaved the sword as far as she could throw, out into the white sky of dawn over the dark curves of the ocean. The blade flickered as it spun in the morning sunlight and then made a slight splash on the surface. Then there was nothing—no *yani*, no shouting, no boat, no sword—just the crashing of the waves against her legs and the chatter of noddy birds overhead, flying out to sea.

'And I will throw this,' said the old man and he tossed the bucket of bones and the tin out to sea with all the gracefulness of a fisherman casting a net.

thirty-two

The Witch Track
Saturday 3 July 2004

They started the walk home in silence, heads down and weary. Hector's mind spun with dozens of questions after watching the scene at the channel. Christina walked a little to the side, chewing her fingernails. She was obviously as confused as he was. Lily looked miserable. Her eyes were troubled and she stumbled a few times as she walked.

The silence began to bother Hector. He knew Lily and Ibu were somehow connected to the whole drama, and even though they were both drained and deserved some peace, Hector had to sort it out in his own mind.

'You were there, weren't you, Ibu. That man was bashing you?' he asked.

The old man waited before replying. 'Yes, it was my past you saw today.'

'Why did we see it?' Christina asked.

'Ghosts walk at night, but they walk more at sunrise and sunset.'

'But I've never seen them before,' Hector said.

'You never have. Some people, like Lily, can see. Some people cannot.'

'So why did I see them today, heaps of them: lepers, marines, men on the reef? I saw them and I saw *you* with them.'

'And I saw them too,' Christina said, shaking her head. 'And shit, I don't know…it must have been real but…how could it be? How did it happen?'

'There was powerful magic today. Two shamans and the black stone, it made a strong picture, for everyone to see.'

'What do you mean, two shamans?'

'The old magic, boy. It's your turn to use it next.'

'Magic…like Gilbertese magic?'

Riki smiled. 'Our magic and the magic of our ancestors,' he said.

They walked on while more questions brewed in Hector's mind. Something about the black stone bothered him. He felt for it in his pocket, its surface was smooth and warm. 'But the stone was with the tin and the body,' he said. 'How did it get there?'

Lily answered for him, looking at Riki as they walked, 'You put it there, didn't you? Long ago.'

The old man chuckled at them. 'Yes, I did it. The black stone sat on Egirow, his tin. It hid him. He worshipped there, with his little book. But the forest ate up the book. My magic, it hid Egirow.'

They came to a junction in the path, turned left and made their way down the hill towards Hector's hut.

'I don't understand. It hid *egirow*—it hides anger?' Hector said.

'That is what we called him, the Lieutenant, the one who bashed me.'

'Yes, the *yani*, Hector. The skull you found, that was Egirow,' said Lily.

'But he wasn't hidden, I found him.'

'Yes, the young shaman found what I had hidden.'

'How did he die?' Christina asked.

The old man stopped and paused before he spoke. 'During the war...' he began.

But Lily couldn't wait for the long build up to the story. 'You killed him, didn't you?' she said, clapping him on the back.

'*Suh!*' Hector blurted out, furious that she'd said something so rude, but his grandfather smiled at them.

'Yes, I did it. I was angry too. I was angry because they killed my brother and because he tricked me, he made me kill my love.'

'Who was she, that girl?' Hector said.

'Her name was Edouwe.'

Lily grabbed at the old man's hand. 'It was Edouwe? It was my auntie?'

Riki nodded and began to walk on. His eyes watered at the mention of her name.

'She called you Tepu,' Lily said.

'Tepu is the start of my name, Tepuariki,' he said.

'I don't understand,' Christina said, 'the marine killed her, you didn't.'

'Two times I tried to save her, two times I sent her to

die. I thought the people at the hospital were safe. But they took them, made us force them onto the boat. I thought we would die together in the boat. But he was cruel, he made me live. We thought the people would float for a few days, then sink, or perhaps someone would rescue them. Then boom! Everyone died. They blew up the boat. And Edouwe, she died in the water but I wanted to be with her. If I was with her, maybe she would have lived.'

Riki turned to Lily and took her stained hand. 'That's why you're special. You have her scar. You are here to heal the past. You helped me do that today.'

'Sometimes I hear her cry, some mornings when I wake,' Lily said. Hector could see her eyes shining with tears as she spoke.

'She calls you, to wake up and heal her, heal the past. I think you'll hear her no more now.'

Hector jostled for position in front of his *ibu* as they walked. He wanted to know more about the ghost. 'How did you kill him, Ibu?' he asked.

The old man sighed again. 'For three days I was sore from the beating. On the fourth day I went in the night to his secret place. It was Egirow's secret place. A place to rest, to hide, to worship. I don't know. No other marine went there. It was his secret but I knew it and I waited and I took the black stone.

'Just before dawn Egirow came and hid inside the pinnacles. I waited to surprise him when he came out but the bombers came too. Boom, boom, boom. I covered my ears. Then there was a big one, so big the ground shook and stones flew down on me. More bombs landed further away. I heard him cry out and I came slowly, into the clearing, but bushes and trees all about were smashed and filled the clearing. He was not in the secret place; he must have run away. I heard another cry and I saw him down the hill, lying down. He moved his legs and tried to crawl but a big bean tree was on his back, holding him. I took a piece of rock to smash his head and he saw me come. I saw his eyes hate me, but before he could shout I smashed his mouth and blood came out. I took his sword because his hand couldn't reach it. I poked the sword in his neck, like I killed a pig and blood sprayed out. He was dead.

'I cut at the tree, and cut at him, and threw bits around the site, like I sliced bait for fishing. But I took his head and some bones and I buried them at the entrance to the secret place. Then I made the magic with the stone and I put it on his tin, to stop him speaking now he's dead. And I knew they'd find him and they'd say the bomb killed him, but they would never find all the pieces and it was me that made him a ghost.'

'So how come no one found him?' Hector said.

'I buried his spirit, the sword, further down the hill.'

'So when we found the sword, he was released from your magic?' Lily said.

'Yes, but he couldn't speak,' Hector added.

'So why did he speak and say Baringa Bay?' she asked.

'The sword was with him again and when Hector took the stone, I called to Egirow. I broke the spell.'

'But why did he want to go to Baringa Bay?' Christina asked.

'He knew that was where he hurt me most. He knew I wanted to go with Edouwe, to die in the open sea. So that was where he should be now. Him instead of me.'

'So it really was an evil thing,' Lily said. 'I thought you were just saying that, to make me throw it away, but it really was the spirit of a cruel man.'

'Yes, but because I became cruel like him, I was ashamed, a coward, and my magic was like a curse. I told no one, except you three.'

'But you weren't a coward, Ibu. You fought back,' Hector said.

'I wanted to kill him, but I killed him like he was an injured dog. I didn't fight fair. That's not a shaman. That's a coward.'

'I don't think the Japanese fought fair, either,' Christina said.

'It's not a bad secret, Ibu. And people will think you *were* brave because you tried to save Edouwe. You can tell people about it now because it's so long ago,' Hector said.

'No, it's not for everyone to hear,' he said and he squeezed Lily's hand and reached out for Hector's also. 'It's our secret. It binds our families. Let it be a gift to them only if they're ready, when they suffer and hurt and need to know their past.'

Hector nodded and looked across at Lily. She winked at him. He blushed as he thought of the love between his *ibu* and Edouwe.

The old man stopped walking. 'I am tired,' he said, 'go on ahead and make us all some tea, then we can rest too. After a long night.'

'You can come and stay at my place for a few days, Lily. Dad won't mind. At least until I go back to Australia next week,' Christina said. She smiled and clasped Lily's hand.

'Thank you,' Lily said. 'And Riki, one day, if you don't mind, I'll go home and tell my mum about your secret.'

Lily looked down at her left hand. It tingled. She was stained, just like the girl's arm was stained with blood, the blood of a desperate soul, a soul that had run through her on the reef, that had been a part of her. A great wisdom and sense of connection flowed over her. Her stain was not a dirty mark, it was a symbol of belonging, a link to the past.

acknowledgments

Thank you Arnold Zable for your inspiration, and to Heather Tobias, Richard Kentwell and John Irving for your encouragement.

To the workshop teams at WWW and Berwick, your comments were invaluable.

Thanks to Penny Hueston for her expert care and critical eye. But most importantly, thank you Jeffter, my husband, for your unceasing support and belief in me.